THE FLAMES ROARED THROUGH THE FARMER'S HOUSE

"This should help scare the settlers out," Frank LaWall chuckled. The job hadn't taken long. They soaked a stack of dried hay behind the house with kerosene and three matches did the rest.

Jib Hobson watched the house burst into flames. He heard LaWall's chuckle and forced himself to laugh with the rest of the gang. But inside him, there was only hate.

A man was in that house—a farmer like Jib Hobson himself. Jib had warned the farmers about LaWall's plan. But something had gone wrong, and now a man was dead.

And Jib Hobson had one more score to settle.

MAD RIVER GUNS

Lee Floren

MB
A MACFADDEN-BARTELL BOOK

THIS BOOK IS THE COMPLETE TEXT
OF THE HARDCOVER EDITION

A MACFADDEN BOOK 1965

MACFADDEN BOOKS are published by
Macfadden-Bartell Corporation
205 East 42nd Street, New York, New York, 10017

Copyright, 1950, by Crestwood Publishing Co., Inc. All rights reserved. Published by arrangement with the author. Printed in the U.S.A.

CHAPTER 1

COLONEL HENRY S. BRADEN was angry. He sat in his swivel-chair, fat forearms resting on his glass-topped desk, and pounded. A vein stood out like a rope across his wide forehead. Lanky Buck McKee, slouched in a chair, looked absently at the enlarged vein and wondered if it would not burst some day. His Mexican partner, squat Tortilla Joe, hunkered with his ox-like back to the wall, chewing on a cold *tortilla* and scowling.

"It's got to stop!" Colonel Henry S. Braden pounded on the open letter on his desk. "Here I send a construction crew into Mad River Basin—after I get the government's backing to build that irrigation project—and here I am, all crippled up——" He accidentally bumped the cast on his right leg against his desk. "Oh, my leg—the pain——"

Buck McKee rolled a cigarette. He stuck it between his thin lips, dug into a vest pocket for a match. He and Tortilla Joe had fought under Colonel Henry S. Braden in the Spanish-American war, now two years dead. They had seen similar explosive scenes on San Juan Hill, on Bataan. Underneath, the Colonel was a good man and good soldier, but sometimes his temper led him astray.

Tortilla Joe looked at Buck. "The colonel, he quiet down soon, Buck," he said. "Purty soon he run outa wind, no?"

Colonel Henry S. Braden stopped short in the middle of a curse. His large mouth hung suspended, his walrus moustaches bristling. "What was that statement, Tortilla Joe?" he demanded.

Tortilla Joe shrugged his massive shoulders. "I just say to Buck here that the weather, she ees too hot, no?"

Buck stretched out his right leg and stroked a match to life on his levis. He regarded the colonel over the jagged flame. "Let's get down to brass tacks, Colonel," he said. "Three days ago me an' Tortilla Joe were over in Dog Town, a hundred miles north of here. Somehow, you heard we was there—so you wrote for us to come hell-for-the-applecart——We got in town an hour ago. We ate and then came out here to your office. This don't set my stomach too well 'specially after eatin' that Chink's boiled son-of-a-gun-in-a-sack."

"*Si*," put in Tortilla Joe. "*Your* laig—what you do to heem, huh? He ees busted plenty, *no esberdad?*" He looked stupidly at the colonel's crutches leaning against his desk.

Colonel Henry S. Braden swallowed, held his anger down. "You know where Mad River is?" he demanded.

Tortilla shrugged.

Buck frowned. "Over across the border in Arizona territory, I think. I've heard tell of it, but never happened to be over in that direction. Somewhere in the *Sangre de Maria* mountains, ain't it?"

The colonel beamed. "That's the location, Buck; about a week or so ride from here, I understand. Well, here's the deal. I sent for you boys because I need help—and need it bad. Things are going to pot over on Mad River."

Buck regarded his boots carefully. He did not know what was *going to pot*, but he judged it was evidently a construction crew that was, according to the colonel's earlier words, building an irrigation project, presumably in Mad River basin.

The colonel's eyes were sharp. "You're my friends, aren't you?"

Tortilla Joe nodded. He said, "Why ask that?"

Buck spoke. "Let's get to the point, Colonel, and get this over with."

Colonel Henry S. Braden got slowly to one foot, bracing himself on his desk while he got his crutches under him. Then he hobbled over to the big map on the wall. He held a yardstick in one hand. He ran the point of it around the map and then settled it on one particular spot.

"This is us—here. Rimrock, New Mexico." The yardstick travelled west slowly, stopped at another point. "Here is the headwaters of Mad River. Up here in the

Sangre de Marias. See where the river spreads out here, and builds Mad River basin? That valley is twenty miles wide. These mountains here and here——" The yardstick travelled north and south. "—are pretty high and they have a good watershed. No, my men aren't damming the Mad River; they're building check dams back against the mountains."

Buck nodded. "They run cattle in there? Run them down there on the flat land? What kind of land is that basin?"

The colonel lifted a freckled hand. "Not so fast, McKee, not so fast. Sure, they run cattle here—the N Bar S, a big outfit owned by Frank LaWall. Of course, Frank LaWall doesn't like the idea of the government turning this into farming land, because it pushes his cattle out——"

Buck finished. "And he's fightin' your men, huh?"

Colonel Henry S. Braden balanced his crutches, dug into his pocket and came out with a brilliant red bandanna. He shook this out and mopped his sweat-covered forehead. "And he's whipping them, I guess."

Buck caught the drift then. The colonel wanted him and Tortilla Joe to ride to Mad River, straighten things out for the construction crew. And Buck knew too well what that meant. He sighed audibly.

"That'll mean trouble, Colonel," he murmured. "And me, I'm gettin' tired of trouble—I've seen too much of it, in the war and out."

Tortilla Joe considered scowlingly. "But it would mean looking at some new territory, Buck. Me, I say we have been too long in one place—thees last job we have held up for almost five months, no?" He counted on his dark fingers. "Almos' seex month," he corrected.

The colonel was watching them so intently he let one crutch slide. He stepped on his bum foot, jerked his crutch back and started to curse again. Buck waited patiently; Tortilla Joe searched his pockets for a cigarette. Buck watched him and then tossed him his sack of Durham.

"Horse fell on me," said the colonel brusquely. "Almost a week ago now, I guess. Broke my tibia."

"Tibia," echoed Tortilla Joe. "What she ees that, Colonel? Once I have a girl that name—down in Jalisco."

"You mean Lydia," corrected Buck.

"Oh, yeah . . . Lydia."

The colonel felt his anger rise again; he was sure Buck and Tortilla Joe were just trying to make a fool out of him. He wished he were their superior officer in the army again—he'd put them to shovelling manure and yard-birding the mules, and when they ran out of that job they could start digging latrines. But they were out of the army now, and he was on the reserved officer list——

"The tibia," he explained "is the inner bone of the leg, running from the knee to my ankle." He winced in pain. "If not farther. . . ." He crutched his way to his chair. "I trust you boys implicitly. I like you and I call you my friends. Not that I mean to impose on our friendship —no, not that."

McKee was wooden-faced as a Cheyenne buck; Tortilla Joe scowled and chewed as he looked at his cigarette. Buck and he had made plans before they came to see the colonel. They had agreed to play dumb and inattentive to increase the colonel's wrath. Whatever the colonel wanted them to do, they would be against it.

Buck said, "I ain't forgettin' that time you made me clean two hundred rifles just because I had a button off in inspection."

"An' me," put in Tortilla; "I have to dress all those turkey-gooses we stole—I mean, we get from natives—— Feefty of them, there was, too."

Colonel Henry S. Braden's jowls fell. "Part of army discipline, boys," he soothed. "Part of my duties as your commanding officer, your superior officer. Not something to take into civilian life, my boys. Needs be, I could recite some little incident whereby I saved you some trouble, made life lighter for you."

"You have to theenk hard," said Tortilla Joe.

The colonel tried a new angle. "There's a good pay in this for both of you," he stated. "Of course, if you don't want to earn it——"

Tortilla Joe's dark eyes lighted. *"Como mucho?* How much?"

"One hundred and fifty per month, apiece."

Tortilla Joe opened his mouth. They had been getting fifty and beans punching cows. But Buck McKee cut in. "Not enough to risk life and limb, Colonel."

Colonel Henry S. Braden stared at him. Buck could see a new storm gathering behind the Colonel's pale eyes.

By deliberate effort the colonel shoved the clouds back and made his eyes smile.

"Of course, if you don't want those wages——"

Buck got to his feet. Tortilla Joe got up lazily and stretched. "We go," he said. "We plenty glad to meet you again, Colonel."

"Two hundred," shouted the colonel.

Buck stopped, hand on doorknob. He looked questioningly at Tortilla Joe. Tortilla Joe considered, shook his heavy head. Buck said, "No," and opened the door.

"Two twenty-five!" the colonel hollered. "Two fifty!"

Buck stopped, turned. Tortilla Joe grunted, sat down again. Buck leaned against the wall. "You hired two men," he said.

Again the lurid bandanna rose, mopped the sweaty forehead. "And I thought you boys were my friends. . . . Two money-mad bloodsuckers who would put friendship aside for money." Anger swelled the rope-like vein again. "I oughta throw you out of here, even if I have a bum leg."

Buck winked at Tortilla Joe. "He's mad again," he said.

"He should go on Mad River. Mad man of Mad River." The fat Mexican's big belly shook with chuckles. "But we got them wages high, no?"

The bandanna stopped in mid-stroke. Colonel Henry S. Braden suddenly understood they were fooling him. He swallowed hard, his Adam's apple bobbing. He sat down gingerly. "If you boys were in the army I'd——"

"But we're not," said Buck.

"Then you'll go?"

Buck grinned. "You ol' nanny goat, we'd go to hell for you. You did it for us, down there in Cuba. How are those old bullet holes in your ribs, anyway? They were meant for me, but you shoved me down in that ditch and took them yourself."

"Ache a little sometimes, Buck." Colonel Henry S. Braden was smiling widely. "Hell, fellow, I never saved your life, you just talk that way." The smile left the army man. "Boys, I'm behind the eight-ball, sure enough. You see, I got the right from the Interior Department to build these dams on Mad River range, and already some settlers have proven up on homesteads, or have homestead shacks built and line fences staked out. And this cowman, Frank

LaWall, and a foreman of his, Dusty Jacobson—well, they got punchers and they haven't any scruples for law and order, I guess."

"Who's boss of your teamsters?" asked Buck.

Colonel Henry S. Braden looked out the window thoughtfully. "A relative of mine, Sin Braden, is boss of the outfit."

"Sin," echoed Tortilla Joe, giving the *e* a broad accent. "That ees an odd name, Seen."

"Short for Sinbad," said Buck drily.

Colonel Henry S. Braden smiled widely. "We'll let it ride at that. I suppose you boys will start soon, huh?"

"In the morning," said Buck. "We'd like to get a good night's sleep first; we been hittin' the saddle rather long hours of late. Come daylight we'll pull out, Colonel."

"I'll be over just as soon as I can ride," said Colonel Henry S. Braden. "But you boys are welcome to stay here, Buck. Got the whole upstairs vacant—the Missus is over at Santa Fe, visiting my daughter there. The girl just had a new baby."

Buck smiled. "Thanks, Colonel, but if we stayed here, you'd get us drunk." The colonel was an ardent foe of alcohol.

"Humph. . . ."

They went outside. The colonel hollered, "Your checks'll be mailed to you each month, or else Sin can credit you for two-fifty each thirty days. Pay starts right now and——" His voice trailed off as Buck and Tortilla swung into leather.

They rode into town, a quarter-mile or so away. They racked their broncs in the town livery and went into the Cinch Ring Saloon. Buck ordered whiskey straight and Tortilla Joe took *tequila*. The Mexican held his glass high.

"To Colonel Braden, Buck."

They drank. Tortilla Joe wiped his mouth with the back of his hand. "I wonder what she ees make the colonel such an enemy of wheeskey, huh?"

"Maybe it makes him sick," said Buck. He motioned to the bartender. "Another snort, white-aprons."

"Feel mine again, too," said Tortilla Joe.

CHAPTER 2

THEY CAME out on a plateau and the wild, disordered land lay below them, pitching off and falling down with the tiny ribbon of Mad River roaring along its bottom, some half-a-mile or so distant.

Buck's tired bronc stood with one hip lower than the other. "Well," drawled Buck, "I guess this is it, Tortilla ... Mad River."

Tortilla Joe's heavy body was deep between horn and cantle on his El Paso saddle. "Tough lookin' land," he muttered. "Ees that a town down there, Buck? See, about ten miles away—in the middle of the valley?"

"Braden was tellin' me about that town," said Buck. "Said they called it Oxbow, and that it is the central trading point for the valley. Yonder is a wagon road; see it running along the river? Comes in that break in the *Sangre de Marias* and meanders over the ridge to Tucson, I reckon. Accordin' to the colonel, a stage comes in once a week ... if'n it's on time."

"Those buildin's beyon' the town—next to the heels? What are they, Buck? Aren't they the buildin's of the N Bar S, thees cowoutfit that belongs to thees *hombre,* Frank LaWall?"

Buck's gaze travelled across more sagebrush. "Yeah, I reckon that's the N Bar S, accordin' to the colonel's description of Mad River basin. Fact is, it's the only sizeable group of buildings outside of Oxbow."

Across the still air they could see tiny puffs of dust hanging against the backdrop of the hills. Buck studied these and scowled. "Them sure look like Injun smoke signals," he finally said. "But hell, the Injuns are out of here an' them that aren't, they're peaceful. Are they dust or are they smoke—and what are they?"

Tortilla scowled, and bit his lip. "Me, I dunno, Buck. But they look like dust, I theenk."

Buck suddenly understood. "That's dust raised by the

fresno's an' teams of the colonel's, a-buildin' them check dams." He counted them carefully. "I see eight of them; that means they are workin' on eight dams."

Tortilla Joe was thoughtful. "Well," he finally said, "we have to get down on this Mad Reever basin, huh? But how? The cliffs below us—we cannot go down them. Our horses slide and beengo—eento the reever they go!"

Buck studied the precipices that tumbled down and levelled out on the floor of the basin. Evidently there was a way to get down, but the trail must have been farther west. They rode west accordingly, travelling on the edge of the rimrock. They rode for a few miles and then they came on a well-travelled trail, heading east and leading up out of the valley.

"This is it, Tortilla."

Their sweat-streaked horses grudgingly took the downward trail sliding on the steeper spots. They were sore-footed despite being shod and their shoulders were stiff, due to the rough terrain they had covered. Therefore this steep downward path made them grunt in protest.

The trail wound around sandstones and boulders, twisting in and out of the canyon. Once they scared two black-tail mule-deer out of the chamiso and cat-claw. The deer bounded away on stiff legs, flags up. Farther on, they scared four head of cattle—a cow, a calf and two steers—out of some rosebushes. They wheeled, snorting, their eyes wild. Then they broke through the thick buckbrush, running wildly. Buck saw they bore Frank LaWall's N Bar S iron.

"How in hades does he round up them cattle," wondered the tall rider. "He must get eagles to chase them outa the brush. No man on horseback could do that. Or else he traps them in corrals."

"They are hees cattle," reminded Tortilla Joe philosophically. "Why should we worry about hees stock, Buck?"

Buck smiled. "I'm not worried, *compadre*."

They reached the foot of the first grade and came to the level plateau. Across this ran the trail for about a hundred yards before it took another downward dip. Here the cottonwood trees and buckbrush was very high.

Buck touched spurs to his horse. Taking the lead, he loped across the mesa, with Tortilla Joe galloping behind him. When they loped through the clump of young cottonwoods, suddenly Buck's bronc stumbled. Hurriedly, Buck pulled up hard, but the horse went down, rolling over. Buck slid from saddle, and the horse went completely over, getting up to stand and tremble.

He figured that the tired horse had fallen over a boulder. But Tortilla Joe's bronc was also down, throwing the Mexican into the brush. Suddenly Buck saw the rope tied across the trail about a foot high. Anchored between two sturdy cottonwoods, the hard twist had tripped their broncs, throwing them.

Buck reached for his gun.

"Don't pull that cutter!" rasped a harsh voice. Two men came out of the brush, their .45's level in their fists.

Buck scowled, drew his hand up, slowly got to his feet. The fall had put a lot of aches in him, and his temper was not too calm. He glanced at Tortilla Joe. The Mexican still sat flatly, his huge face showing surprise.

Both of the men were big. But the red-haired one—a man of about forty-five—was the bigger. He stood wide-legged, his eyes small on either side of his hawkish nose, his lips bearing a twisted smile.

The other was a dark-haired, thick-lipped man, wearing Cheyenne-leg chaps and spurs using Mex pesos for rowels. His holster was tied low against his heavy thigh. A horse had evidently kicked him in the face at one time. His nose was twisted, crooked; the left side of his forehead had been smashed in, was now lower than the other side.

The red-head said, "I'm Frank LaWall, owner of the N Bar S. This hairpin is my segundo, Dusty Jacobson. Now who t'hades are you two hellions—and what's your business on Mad River?"

Buck growled. "Is this the way you greet a man in your country? Tie a rope across the trail an' bust him an' his bronc? Someday some hand will teach you gents a lesson—a gun-lesson——"

"Won't be you two," growled Dusty Jacobson.

Buck glared at the N Bar S foreman. "Now don't be too sure of that, Jacobson!" Tortilla Joe knew his partner and, knowing Buck, he knew there would be trouble ahead. He decided to avert it. He got to his feet, wiping the dust from his pants. "We no want troubles, *senores*.

We ees just ride through thees Mad Reever co'ntry, goin' to other side an' then out across the mountains."

"Your handles?" growled Frank LaWall.

The Latin shrugged, spread his dark hands. "Me, I am Tortilla Joe, the Mexican—an' these hombre she ees my partner, Buck McKee." He trusted that neither LaWall nor Jacobson had heard of him and Buck.

LaWall scowled. "Strangers to me," he admitted. "How about you, Jacobson?"

"Never heard of the sons before," muttered Jacobson.

Tortilla Joe felt his muscles loosen. "We jus' ride across the valley," he repeated. "That okay with you?"

LaWall holstered his gun, smiling a little. "Well, now, looks like we acted too hasty, men," he said apologetically. "But there's been a mite of trouble here on Mad River. Fact is, the sodbusters are tryin' to shove me an' my N Bar S stock out and run irrigation in to raise crops. So me an' Dusty here figured you two was sodbusters, so we figured we'd greet you proper——"

Dusty Jacobson smiled, too. He also holstered his piece. "Danged sorry we upset a couple of cowpunchers. Now that things are kinda soothed down, how about tyin' up with the N Bar S?"

"Gun-slammer wages," murmured Frank LaWall. "Two hundred and found and ten dollars for each gun ruckus, fifty if you kill a Braden homesteader or construction hand. Cash on the line, no checks."

Buck spoke slowly. "Well, we didn't intend to——"

Tortilla Joe cut in. "We think eet over, LaWall."

"Better make up your minds pronto," snapped Frank LaWall. "This outfit calls for action, not for thought. Are you or ain't you?"

Buck balanced himself carefully on the balls of his Justins. He had held his anger long enough. He said huskily, "We ain't——" and he struck. His fist crashed against Frank LaWall's heavy jaw. Startled more than stunned, LaWall stepped back, reaching for his gun. Buck smashed in a right and left and LaWall sat down, stupidly.

Buck turned suddenly, gun out. But Dusty Jacobson was out of the play; he stood with Tortilla Joe's hogleg in his ribs. Buck reached down and snagged LaWall's gun from leather.

"Now get up!" he ordered.

Tortilla Joe took Dusty Jacobson's gun. "I've deesarmed thees beeg son," he said, grinning widely.

LaWall gathered his legs under him and got up rubbing his jaw slowly. Gradually sanity returned to his green eyes. "What's the play?" he mumbled.

Buck spoke clearly. "No scissorbill is goin' to hoolyhan me an' my partner an' get away with it!" He gestured with his gun. "You move over here, Jacobson." Then, over his shoulder to Tortilla Joe, "They've got their broncs cached around here somewhere. Find them, Joe."

"Si, Buck."

Tortilla Joe waddled his obese bulk into the buckbrush. "You'll pay to me for this," growled Frank LaWall. "And what's more, McKee, you'll pay through the schnozzle, and pay plenty."

"Talk's cheap," reminded Buck. "Takes cold cash to buy whiskey."

"What do you aim to do?" asked Dusty Jacobson.

Buck grinned with his lips only. "You'll find out." He raised his voice. "Tortilla you find their cayuses yet?"

"I find them now, Buck."

Tortilla came out of the buckbrush leading a dun and a sorrel. Buck told him to strip the saddles and bridles from the broncs and turn them loose. Dusty Jacobson's eyes were sharp and Frank LaWall spat out an oath.

"You mean to make us walk back into town," he roared. "Hades, man, that's all of ten miles!"

"Walk off some of that big gut of yours," said Buck.

Tortilla Joe slapped the horses over the rumps with a bridle. They loped away, tails up, tearing through the brush. They could never be caught by a man on foot. A few minutes later, they were out of sight around a bend in the trail.

"Look them over for hideout guns," said Buck.

Tortilla Joe cleverly frisked the two irate cowmen. "They ain't got no other guns, Buck." His grin was wide on his thick lips. "By the time they tote them saddles eento town, they weel be tired *muchachitos,* no?"

"Yes," agreed Buck.

"You stay in Mad River valley and one of us will kill you!" growled Frank LaWall. "Ride right through and save your hides, you tinhorns!"

"He ees angry," said Tortilla Joe, shrugging. "Now

why for what would he be mad about, Buck? Ees eet that he leeve too close to Mad Reever, that he ees mad too?"

"He'll be madder yet when he finds out we aim to work for Sin Braden," said Buck.

Frank LaWall held back his temper. "You mean you —*two cowpunchers*—are goin' work for Sin Braden an' the sodbusters?"

"Sad, but true," said Buck. "Never have heard tell of two cowpokes to fall that low, huh?"

LaWall's green eyes glistened. "That means we get another whack at them, Dusty. Maybe this ain't goin' turn out so bad, at that. . . ."

But Dusty Jacobson was not so optimistic. "It's a long way into town," he said, "an' my saddle'll be awful heavy. . . ."

Buck and Tortilla mounted and loped off. They went for about five miles, and then they hit the level ground— here they heard hoofs cutting in from their right. Buck pulled in, hand on gun, and searched the chamiso and malapai, a frown on his forehead.

"You don't suppose them two caught their broncs?"

Tortilla Joe also had his hand on his weapon. "That would be eempossible, Buck. Look, a monkey comes over the heel, an' he rides a horse!"

"A monkey!"

Buck stared. The horse was an iron-grey gelding, a big horse. And the rider, perched bareback on the beast, was a bent-over gnome who, from a distance, looked sure enough like a monkey. But when the horse came closer, Buck could make out the features of the man—he was only about five feet tall, weighing about ninety pounds. He wore a breech-cloth and moccasins and he had a rawhide band tied around his head to hold back his stringy black hair.

"No monkey," muttered Tortilla Joe. The Latin crossed himself hurriedly. "What ees he, Buck? The devil, no?"

Buck said, "Looks like an Injun to me."

The gnome raised his right hand high, palm out—the sign of peace in the sign-language. Buck and his partner raised their hands, too. The gnome guided his big horse by a maguey rope around his bottom jaw.

"Me Dondo," he said.

Buck spoke. "We ride through. Who is Dondo?"

A scowl showed on the wrinkled, brown face. Small beady eyes were sharp against them. "Dondo chief, Ilaks. Apache tribe."

Buck had heard of the Ilaks. A branch of the Apache tribe, they had centuries before moved back on Mad River, settled down and become farmers, not fighters. Once the Navahos had swept through this region killing most of the Ilaks off. Buck spread his hand wide. That meant: How many in your tribe?

Dondo grinned. "Two men, me and Pone. Three women, our women, all that is left. Rest—go to hell. Leave basin." His grin was mischievous. "You fellows come—help Sin Braden?"

Buck stared. "How did you know?"

"Me hide in brush. Hear you say to LaWall, Jacobson. Glad to see you hit them. Me, I jus' ready to help, you hit. Dondo like Sin Braden. He work for Sin. Work like sin for Sin."

"What you do now?" asked Tortilla Joe.

"Me ride to Sin. Tell about you come. You go to town first, huh?"

"We're hungry," said Buck. "We'll be out later. Where's the main camp?"

Speaking abruptly, Dondo told them. Then he turned his grey, thundered off, perched on the huge beast, hanging onto the thick mane.

Tortilla Joe looked at Buck. "What she ees next, huh?"

"Search me," said Buck.

CHAPTER 3

OXBOW WAS a town that consisted of three business houses: a combined post-office and stage depot, a general store with a whiskey bar, and a small shack that bore the battered sign: *deputy sheriff's office*. One thing the town did have—and that was some shade, a welcome relief from the stern sun.

Buck and Tortilla Joe pulled up under a cottonwood. "Hell of a lookin' town," grunted Buck slowly. "Which place do we look over first, *compadre?*"

"We can start at one end, take each buildin' as she comes to us." Tortilla Joe stepped down and their horses nibbled some grass at the base of the big tree. A cur bounced stiffly out of the post-office, stopped suddenly, decided the sun was too hot, and trotted back inside. "That would put us in the shereef's office first."

Buck smiled. "Might be a good idea to look over the law."

The deputy was an old gent of about sixty-five. Bow-legged, stooped, he was homely, with a long grey beard. Buck got the impression that he resembled a goat very strongly. His whining voice was almost a bleat, too.

"You gents N Bar S hands?"

Buck replied. "Wouldn't be caught dead on the N Bar S. We came to side Sin Braden, grandpappy."

"Nappy's the name, fella. Nappy Hale. Ma named me after Napoleon, I reckon. Born about that time." He paused, reflected, eyes shiny with thought. "Nope, I come after Napoleon's death, I reckon. Died in about 1820, didn't he, Mexican?"

"Never heard of him," said Tortilla Joe. "Who was he, a cowboy?"

"Trouble here," said Nappy Hale.

Buck offered him some smoking. He took the tobacco in trembling fingers. "So we understand," said Buck. He told the oldster that he and Tortilla Joe had been commissioned to aid Sin Braden, on request of Henry S. Braden. There was no use in keeping anything secret. Sooner or later, the basin would find out why he and Tortilla Joe were on Mad River, and it might just as well be now as later, he figured.

"Already we feexed thees LaWall an' his *hombre*, thees Dusty," grinned Tortilla Joe. He told about the fight out there on the rimrock.

Old Nappy's eyes widened. "Hades, younker," he breathed, "you'll be marked in the book—both of you— in red ink."

"You've been forced to make any arrests?" asked Buck.

Gnarled fingers tremblingly twisted a paper around some tobacco. "Me, I don't hol' this office to make any arrests, McKee." Nappy grinned as he saw Buck's eyebrows raise in wonderment. "Come a year or so back, I was a pensioner, drawin' my pension from the county. I got down at the county seat—that's Wishbone, sixty miles south—and my pension was so small I kept hollerin' about it. County commissioners finally met—understand they couldn't give me a higher pension, see? So they made me a deputy, sent me home. Now I get a bigger check an' I don't make their lives miserable."

"Then there's no law on Mad River?" asked Buck.

"No law, McKee. That is, outside of me . . . an' I don't count. . . ."

"You sendin' somebody out to meet LaWall and Jacobson?"

"Hades, no! Jehosaphat, them two hellions think they're so great—Lassrope, they can walk inter town, the ijiouts."

Buck and Tortilla went outside. Buck was smiling a little. "One-third of the town has been visited," he said drily. "Let's go in here." They entered the store. A fat Mexican, his mustachios sharp as pitchfork tines, waddled forward to meet them, his fat face beaming.

"I make wait on you, *senores,*" he said. "What you want in the groceries I have, and what I have in liquor you have."

Buck said, "Two boxes of .45 ca'tridges, Pancho."

"The name, she ees not Pancho," the Mexican corrected. "She ees Franco Gomez, *senor.*" He got the cartridges down from a shelf and blew across the tops of the packages but no dust came. "Oh, I forgot, *hombres.* These boxes they are new—Franco Gomez sells lotsa bullets these days."

Tortilla Joe sniffed. "What ees that I smells, Buck?"

Buck tested the air. "Tortillas," he said.

Franco Gomez smiled widely. "My wife, Peta, she ees cook. Back there she ees run lunch counter." He pointed to the back door. "You are hongrys, no?" He escorted them to the door; he pushed it open. "Peta, customers."

A short-order counter almost filled the small lean-to. The other half was filled by the fat woman and the hot stove. Two little girls played with a dirty baby on the bare floor. The fat woman looked up, wiped the hair from her eyes, then stared at Tortilla Joe. Suddenly she was rushing forward.

"Tortilla, oh, Tortilla Joe." She flung her arms around the stolid Tortilla and planted a huge kiss on his dusty cheek. "What you do here, Tortilla?" She buried her head on his shoulder and hid her face. Tortilla patted her broad back and smiled widely at Buck.

"My ol' girl-frien'," he said. "Down in Sonora, seex years or so ago, I guess. We almos' got married, remember."

"There's been too many of them," said Buck.

Franco Gomez's eyes were smaller and his smile had disappeared. "You were in love with Peta, huh? Now she ees my wife—*madre de mias muchachitos*——" His arm gestured toward the three little children. "—you cannot take her. For you have your arms around her, *senor*."

Peta raised her head, laughing. Tears ran down her fat cheeks. "Do not be so jealous, *Franco mio*. Those times they are gone, I am just happy. You see, he ees a relative of mine, too. What ees eet, Tortilla?"

Tortilla thought. "She ees cousin of my seester-in-law's daughter's youngest seester," he finally said.

Buck sighed audibly. He had seen too much of Tortilla Joe's relatives, shirt-tail or close.

"We have *tortillas*," said Peta, eyes twinkling. "And with them we have *tequila, tambien*. What do you theenk of my babies, Tortilla? Jes' theenk, they could be yours, eef eet were not for your saddlehorse."

Tortilla frowned. "Why my horse?"

"He carry you away from me."

Buck drawled, "Sometimes a horse does come in darned handy," and they all laughed. The meal was delicious. Tortillas and frijoles and fried cactus. The cactus, Peta stressed, grew in the backyard. She had climbed the ladder herself and cut it from the stalk. She had then skinned it, taking the barbs off.

"Good," said Tortilla Joe, his cheeks bulging.

An hour later, they entered the post-office. The postmaster was a wiry, middle-aged man with a spade beard. He looked them over with bright eyes and grunted, "Gunfighters, huh? N Bar S hands. . . ."

"You got us wrong," said Buck. "We're workin' for Sin Braden. Have they come in for mail today for the construction camp? Stage came through this mornin', I understand."

"They ain't come in yet, and they got lots of mail." The man hobbled to the window and looked out, grinning. "There comes Frank LaWall an' that two-hit gun-slingin' foreman of his'n, Dusty Jacobson. Walkin' into town from the hills. On foot, that's odd."

"Sure is," said Buck.

He and Tortilla Joe went outside. LaWall and Jacobson were standing there, looking at his horse and Tortilla Joe's. Buck and Tortilla had the guns of the two men tied to their saddle strings. The two cowmen saw the .45's tied there and started toward them, dropping their saddles in the shade of the trees.

Buck said, "Leave those guns alone, you two!"

The two cowmen turned. Buck walked wordlessly toward them. They stopped and stood there, watching him. Frank LaWall's stern face was marked by harsh lines. He pushed back his Stetson and Buck saw the rim of his red hair.

"McKee, I oughta take you apart!"

Buck stopped. "Why don't you?"

Nappy Hale came bowlegging forward, almost running. He shoved his skinny carcass in front of LaWall, his old hogleg pushed into the cowman's belly. "Now none of that, Frank," he panted. "No gun-play, please."

Oxbow's citizenry were out *en masse*. Peta and Franco Gomez, surrounded by their unwashed offspring, stood in front of their establishment. The Postmaster, his wife beside him, watched from that point.

Tortilla Joe stood with his thumbs hooked in his gunbelt. Dusty Jacobson stood to one side, watching closely and fully aware that Tortilla Joe's dark eyes were flatly on him.

"You weel be careful, Tortilla?" said Peta.

Tortilla Joe nodded shortly.

LaWall stepped back. Nappy Hale followed him. LaWall said, finally, "By hades, I guess you would use that gun, huh?" and grinned. He added: "There'll be no trouble, Nappy, unless that fella starts it."

"He won't start any," promised Nappy. "Ain't that so, McKee?"

Buck had to smile. "All right, Nappy."

Nappy holstered his ancient firearm. "You just forget about your guns until Tortilla Joe an' McKee get out of town, LaWall. Hustle over to Peta's an' fill your belly with hot grub. One of your men will come in sooner or later and he can rustle you a coupla horses from the ranch. When you get ready to quit town, your guns'll be in my office."

Frank LaWall and Dusty Jacobson crossed the street and entered Franco Gomez's store. The entire Gomez tribe followed the two inside. Buck just noticed the buckboard that had entered town.

The driver—a heavy-set, middle-aged woman—had pulled the team to a halt in front of the post-office. Beside her on the buggy seat was a thin, slender girl of about twenty-two—a blonde girl with a full, mature figure. The middle-aged woman called, "Hey, Buck! Buck McKee! Come over here, you an' Tortilla!"

Buck stared. Who knew him and Tortilla Joe in this section? He looked at the Mexican, whose big mouth sagged open in surprise.

"Now who's she?" grunted Buck. "Another squaw you almost married?"

Tortilla Joe squinted. "She ees look like Cattle Annie," he said slowly.

Buck said, "By heaven, it is Cattle Annie! Now what do you suppose she is doin' down here in Arizona, Tortilla? Saw her less than a year ago in her saloon up in Colorado." They went to the buckboard.

Cattle Annie was as homely as a woman could be. Scraggly brown hair fell on buckskin clad shoulders. Shrewd brown eyes peered out of a wrinkled face that looked like old leather. She wrapped her arms around Buck and shook him. She grabbed Tortilla and kissed him loudly.

"Buck! Tortilla! What in the——? What are you doin' here, quick!"

"We came to help Sin Braden," said Buck. "Colonel Henry S. Braden sent us."

"You came to help Sin?" Cattle Annie spoke to the girl beside her. "Listen to that, honey! Doesn't that sound good, Janice?" She turned her attention back to Buck and Tortilla Joe. "So you came to help me, huh?"

"Huh," said Tortilla Joe. "We come to help Sin Braden, not you."

Cattle Annie laughed. She slapped her immense thigh

with an open palm. "Listen to that, Janice," she said. "They came to help Sin Braden! Hell, they don't know that I'm Sin Braden!"

Buck stared.

Cattle Annie sobered. "The real name is Cynthia Braden," she explained. "Cattle Annie is just a name I used up in my saloon. I sold that joint and came here to build the irrigation project for the colonel. This is my daughter, Janice."

Janice curtsied.

Buck spat angrily on the ground. "Now why didn't the colonel tell us you were Sin Braden?" he demanded.

Sin Braden smiled widely. "He just wanted to have some fun with you prob'ly. Colonel Henry Braden ain't so dumb, boys."

Tortilla Joe mopped his sweaty forehead. He looked at Janice. "He sure knows how to peeck purty relatives," he said slowly.

CHAPTER 4

CATTLE ANNIE dragged them into Peta's bar, telling that henceforth she would be known as Sin Braden. All of the local people, she said, knew her by that name—she wanted to leave the Cattle Annie name behind.

"Fill 'em up, Franco," she told the grinning Mexican. She spoke to Janice. "Honey, hadn't you better run along?"

"I'm over twenty-one," declared Janice. "I can drink in a bar."

Buck was slightly taken back by this sudden turn of events. The merry-go-round was whirling by and he couldn't grab a hand hold. He and Tortilla Joe had known Sin Braden for a number of years, stopping off now and then at her bar, there at a Colorado outpost.

According to his memory, the woman had four husbands that he knew of. Two of them had died natural deaths, one had run off, and one had been hanged for horse-stealing. His eyes, Sin Braden had said, had been bad. He had not been able to read brands very closely.

Buck studied her. "Where's your husband?" he asked.

The big woman laughed. "Ain't got one, Buck. Nor I won't have one unless Tortilla here marries me!" She pounded the Mexican on his broad back.

"I marry you," said Tortilla, grinning widely. "Like hell...."

"Did you see Dondo?" asked Buck.

Sin Braden told him that Dondo had ridden into the construction camp, told her about himself and Tortilla Joe, so she and Janice had hooked up and driven into Oxbow. And Buck, remembering their lathered team, knew that they had really driven fast.

Frank LaWall and Dusty Jacobson had tossed down a drink, gone into the street again, where they rested on their spur shanks in front of the post-office. Ancient Nappy Hale, squatting in front of his office, had a rifle across his skinny legs, and his sunken eyes regarded the two sharply. Buck remembered that the old star-toter had said he wasn't much of a lawman. Buck knew that the old fellow had just been putting out a spiel to him. Nappy Hale would fight anything he could get at.

"We saw Jib Hobson cuttin' across Swamp crick meadows when we drove in," said Sin Braden. "He's an N Bar S hand. He'll rustle some horses for them two somewhere; prob'ly run up some N Bar S horses out of the brush below town."

"There he comes now," said Janice.

Jib Hobson was a young fellow, about twenty-two or thereabouts. Slim, good-looking, he rode a loose saddle. Buck saw character in the man's face. Hobson had one gun, pulled low. He saw Janice, who had gone to the dirty window, and he lifted one hand slightly. She nodded back.

"One more round," said Sin Braden, "and we head for camp, men."

"I'll go get the mail . . . if there is any," said Janice.

Buck and Sin Braden and Tortilla Joe followed the girl outside. Buck and Tortilla tied their horses behind the buckboard and climbed up on the back seat. Sin turned the team, then waited for Janice.

Janice came from the post-office. "Stage isn't in yet," she said. "Shall we wait?"

Sin looked at Frank LaWall and Dusty Jacobson. She glanced at Buck and Tortilla. Down the street, Nappy Hale was staring at them, his beard lifting and falling as he chewed tobacco.

"You better get them outa town, Sin," acknowledged Nappy Hale. He fell back to chewing. He reminded Buck of a billygoat eating the label from a coffee can.

"Yeah, get out," said LaWall.

Sin said, angrily, "You can't drive me out, LaWall!" She eyed the cowman pointedly. He settled back again against the post-office, grinning. Sin slapped the team with the whip and they rolled out of town, with Buck and Tortilla's saddle-horses trotting behind.

Buck saw a rider off to the north a mile or so. That was Jib Hobson hazing some N Bar S saddle-horses toward Oxbow. There he would corral them and LaWall and Jacobson could get mounted again. He smiled and mentally reviewed his acquaintanceship with the two cowmen; that meeting had been far from pleasant.

They came out of the sagebrush and drove through a prairie-dog town. The dogs barked at them, tails bobbing with their efforts. When they got close the dogs tumbled into their holes. Their barkings were shrill on the thin air. They left the town behind and came to a lane. Barbwire stretched on each side. An irrigation ditch, carrying muddy water, ran along the fence.

Beyond the barbwire was a grainfield. Wheat stood knee-high, billowing and moving in the evening breeze. The sudden movement from a prairie-dog desolation to a green patch of farm land rather amazed Buck. Sin Braden, glancing back at him read his open surprise.

"That's our experimental farm, Buck. We got one check dam finished early and we caught the spring run-off. We're dolin' the water down on this quarter-section. Beyond this wheat is an oat field. Another part is put in barley and another in rye. And with a little water, this desert can raise anything, any crop."

Buck grunted, "It sure looks that way, Sin."

Sin Braden looked across the green field. Buck saw a softness enter her hard eyes. Before she had always seemed hard, calculating. Now, for the first time, he saw her inner character, saw that the other had been just a pose.

She had been unhappy, then; now, with this mighty task ahead of her, she seemed happy.

"Some of the farmers have already come in," she said slowly. "Of course, the real influx hasn't started yet, Buck. When it does, Colonel Henry S. Braden will have men recruiting farmers from back east. We want poor people —people who have little hope in factories, who have farmed in the Old Country—It'll mean a new lease on life for some Hunky or Dago or Frog."

Buck studied the surrounding mountains. "A man could run cattle back there," he said. "Then he could feed his stock grain and fatten them up before trailin' them out of the country. Looks to me like you can't miss. But why doesn't LaWall get wise? Why doesn't he get hold of some of this land?"

Sin nodded. "He has, Buck. He has had his punchers file on homesteads. Then when they have proved up, they'll sell their rights back to him. But that hasn't worked so well, either."

"Yeah?"

"Most of the punchers, after seein' what water did to their desert claims, decided to keep their homesteads. They gave up their saddles and took a plough-handle in their hands. They refused to sell their rights to LaWall. Of course, they are legally right—but you know how that would sit with LaWall."

"Sit on his neck—like a sharp axe. . . ."

But the arrogance and power of a big cow-outfit was strong and demanding. Thousands of head of cattle, jostling and crowding, raising a dust-cloud that reached the sky, their lowing heard for miles . . . Cowpunchers working with blacksnake whips, snapping and cracking: the smell of the branding fires, the stink of a hot iron searing a calf's hide. Cattle needed range and barbwire—The two were incompatible . . . Buck knew all this, and read strife into it.

They were driving along the bank of Mad River. When Buck and Tortilla had crossed the stream, miles back, the water had been rapid but the river had been narrow. Here, with the inflow of a number of creeks, the river was wider.

Buck saw why they called it Mad River. Because of the rapid fall, the river ran very swiftly, dancing over igneous boulders, sending spray as it hurried downward. In many places it became a mad, swirling stream. And over all this energy was the sibilant hiss of the river.

At a number of places, the river spread out slightly, and at these spots the water ran slower, and was not as deep. Here a man and a horse could ford, although the horse would probably have to swim a little. But if the current swung a horse and rider around, sending them into the rapids——

Buck said, "Treacherous river, Sin."

Sin Braden was silent for ten seconds. Then her brown eyes twinkled in her leathery face. "More than the river is treacherous on this range, Buck."

The team trotted on, dust rose. Behind them, the two saddle-horses were rimmed with dust, too. The dust rising from the wheels ahead of them had become smeared with their sweat and gave them a tired, woe-begone look. They were tired, too: they had travelled far and had had little feed.

The road lifted, left the sagebrush, entered scraggly greasewood. They were moving toward the hills to the west. They passed a herd of workhorses grazing on a coulee bottom. The herder lifted his hand. Buck knew these were workhorses used to pull fresnos and ploughs to build the dam. The herder was the nighthawk. His job called that he herd the horses all night and bring them in at daylight for another day of work.

Because of the rise in elevation, the buckboard team had slowed to a long walk. They came around the toe of a rocky hill that was dotted with chamiso clumps and yucca lilies, and the construction camp was in a wide coulee. Tents were spilled along the natural springs of cold water.

There were feed racks for the teams and an oat shed. Behind barbwire was a haystack of native bluestem. Smoke curled up from the cook-tent and the hands were eating outside at the long plank table. Buck smelled the good aroma of boiled beef and spuds and hot coffee.

Racks had been built of cottonwood to hold the harnesses. Fresnos and ploughs were grouped on the base of the hill. And behind all this was the earthen dam. At this stage, it was about twenty feet high, and would go up about ten more feet. Buck asked if there was any water impounded behind it.

"Not much," said Sin. "A little of course. But when

winter comes, and snow melts back in the mountains—it'll fill up."

"Probably too fast," grunted Buck. "You're makin' spillways with each dam, ain't you? Got to have some way for the surplus water to run off, or it'll break your dam an' wash it out."

"We're makin' spillways." Sin pulled the team in and handed the reins to a bewhiskered construction man. "Welcome to Wildcat crick dam, Buck."

Buck jabbed his elbow against Tortilla Joe's ribs. "Wake up."

CHAPTER 5

JIB HOBSON found a small band of N Bar S horses down along Mad River. Mosquitoes had driven them to the brush where they grazed in the lush river grass. He hazed them out of the wild rosebushes and turned them toward Oxbow. He did not drive them fast. LaWall and Jacobson can wait, he thought; the wait will do them good.

The horses were well-broken saddle-stock that had been turned loose when the spring roundup was finished. They trotted into Franco Gomez' corral and LaWall shut the gate behind them.

"You took your time, Jib," said the N Bar S owner.

Hobson regarded him quietly. He was a slow-speaking youngster and he had crammed plenty of living into his twenty odd years. He was playing a dangerous game and death would be his reward if he slipped. "We got a lot of time," he commented.

LaWall walked out with his twine behind him. "Which one do you want, Dusty?"

"That grey, Frank."

The loop sang out, settled around the grey's neck. Dusty Jacobson put his bridle on the beast and took LaWall's rope loose. He led the grey out and the cowman roped a big dun. Then he hazed the rest of the horses back on government range.

The three rode away, Frank LaWall and Dusty Jacobson in the lead, Jib Hobson riding behind them. They loped across the sagebrush, swinging away from Mad River. Jib Hobson listened to the dying song of the swift waters and finally it was submerged into the beat of their hoofs and into the distance.

Off in the distance, LaWall saw a horse and rider, over a mile away. He squinted and said, "Another one of those damned Ilaks. Wonder if this is Dondo or Pone?" He stopped and reached back for his rifle, then remembered he had left it at home. "Wish I had my Winchester."

Jacobson asked, "Why?"

"I'd draw a bead," grinned Frank LaWall. His greenish eyes showed streaks of grey. "I'd pull down on him and knock that damned monkey off'n his horse."

Jacobson drew his forefinger suggestively across his throat. "And get your throat slitted some dark night, huh?"

Jib Hobson grinned faintly. "They can creep through the brush and get past a watch-dog," he said. "They'd cut your throat and you'd never know about it until you were dead. I saw it down over in New Mexico, Frank."

LaWall said, "All right, forget it."

They gained the higher ground and below them they could see Sin Braden's buckboard, crawling along the base of a distant hill. Frank LaWall looked hard across space, and Dusty Jacobson stroked his broken, twisted nose.

"Two hard-cases," murmured the N Bar S *segundo*. "Quick with both fists and guns, and prob'ly here for a gun-job."

LaWall glanced at him. "You sound scared, Dusty," he jibed.

Dusty Jacobson shrugged, was silent. But back of his lack-lustre eyes was a vein of anger. Jib Hobson marked this and wondered if he could ever use it. He stirred in his saddle.

"What do you say, Frank?" he drawled.

LaWall pondered, finally spoke. "There'll come a time when things will break right. Maybe that time will be soon, Jib."

Jib Hobson said, "I want no part of their guns, Frank. I tell you now. I want you to remember it. Unless they force me, I'm not pulling a gun against those two."

"You draw gun-hand wages, Jib."

"Don't care if I do. That's my stand. Take it or leave it."

Frank LaWall held back his temper. He turned his bronc "You're an odd fellow, Jib. Hard to read. Well, there are other places for you to use your gun, I reckon. Let's drift." They rode off, and followed a wagon trail that ran west.

They dismounted in front of the barn and handed their reins to the old *mozo*. Frank LaWall said, "Meet me in the house after chuck." Somebody shouted gleefully and a half-breed boy of about six came running from the big house, hurrying toward Frank LaWall. The big man squatted and caught the boy, holding him close and then lifting him in the air.

"How are you, War Chief?"

"I wait for you, dad."

LaWall went to the house, carrying the boy. His squaw, a heavy-set Navaho, had supper ready, and she started serving it, carrying the hot meal from the big woodstove. LaWall kissed her and hugged her, putting his son on the floor.

"I worry about you," said the squaw. "All the time, Frank, I worry. I wish you would give in, get rid of your cattle—only keep a few. Then you could farm, too. But this way——"

He interrupted her good-naturedly with, "Now Feather Eagle, stop that. That won't get you anything but a lot more worry." He had ridden through a Navaho camp almost ten years before, and he had seen her in front of her sire's tepee. She had been dressing buckskin, chewing the fine leather carefully, and he had stepped down. She had cost him ten fine ponies, but she had been worth it. They had been married at the Santa Ynez mission, and she had left her tribe for good.

"Where were you?" she asked.

"Up along the east trail. We ran into a couple of fellows, and had a little fun." He did not mention that the fellows he had met had had the fun, not himself and Dusty Jacobson.

The meal was good. Corn from the garden; also squash and cucumbers. He ate, his son beside him chattering about his day on the ranch. How he had ridden the old pinto down to the water-hole, and gone swimming.

After supper, he washed the dishes, and War Chief

wiped them. The boy's real name was Frank, too, but his dad called him War Chief as a nickname. The squaw was heavy with child and slow and LaWall had washed the dishes of late to save her the trouble.

They sat for a while on the porch. Finally War Chief's head started to nod; he fell asleep in his chair. His father carried him into his room, undressed him and put him to bed. He glanced into his wife's room. She was in bed, asleep. He went to the horse corral and squatted there beside the cottonwood bars.

Jib Hobson came up. He settled and drew a long forefinger through the dirt. He said, "Hans Sexton just rode in, Frank."

LaWall nodded.

Dusty Jacobson came out of the shadows. He put his husky shoulder against a corral post. "Sexton is here," he said.

"Jib just told me," said LaWall.

Jacobson sat down. He leaned back against the post, chewing his toothpick idly.

"Here comes Hans," murmured Jacobson.

Hans Sexton was a small man. He wore overalls and a rough flannel shirt. An Apache war-axe had once split his nose. Now it had grown together with a red scar, and it twisted and ran to one side. He rubbed the scar carefully and squatted. He said, "Howdy, men."

"Talk," said LaWall.

Sexton shifted, settled back. "They came into camp an hour or so ago. Buck McKee an' Tortilla Joe. They——"

"We know all about them," said LaWall.

Jacobson smiled faintly and spat out his toothpick. His face was dark and without life, and Jib Hobson studied him with a thick indifference. Jib Hobson squatted there and drew his forefinger across the dust. He was thinking of Janice Braden. Her hair was soft and he remembered its healthy aroma. He glanced at the unfathomable night and felt something could move across his spine. It settled there and held him and he wondered what it was. He put his attention back to Hans Sexton.

Sexton rubbed his crooked nose. "They've got guards out around all the dams. Of course, a man could go through the brush and get behind one. . . . But those Injuns keep pretty close watch. Every time you turn around, one of those Ilaks are there. But it could be done, Frank."

"Watch out those Injuns don't trail you over here," warned LaWall. "Not that it would make much difference to me, I could buy off another dirt-mover over in the Braden camp. But it would be hard on your throat."

"My throat," said Hans Sexton.

Frank LaWall moved, a leg muscle tightening. The pain passed and he felt impatience inside again. This was moving too slowly. He decided to speed things up.

"We got to get these farmers out," he said. "The way it looks to me, if one of them got scared good and plenty—the others would hightail out when he went. Hans, you know about these farmers—when will one of them be away from home some night? We could slip in and burn him down to the ground. That would probably scare him into pulling stakes an' goin' back east." He looked at Dusty Jacobson.

Jacobson shrugged. "Might work," he said.

"What do you say, Jib?"

Jib Hobson said, "You're the boss, Frank. You never hired me to think, did you?"

LaWall's eyes tightened.

Hans Sexton said, "Dirty Henry Smutton is going to town day after tomorrow. He'll prob'ly get a few drinks in Franco Gomez' place and bed down under his wagon to sleep off his jag."

Frank LaWall mused. "Smutton, huh. He's the bachelor, ain't he? The middle-aged gent on Runnin' Butte, down on the crick?"

"The gent with the dirty clothes," said Hans Sexton. "Yeah, he's a bachelor—nobody'd marry him, he's so dirty. You get down-wind on him on a hot day an'—He tol' me today he was goin' in day after tomorrow."

"We'll wreck his place," said Frank LaWall.

Dusty Jacobson grunted. "And what if Dirty Henry doesn't go to town . . . and what if he is home when we hit the place?"

"That'll be his tough luck," said LaWall. "What else do you know, Sexton?"

Hans Sexton rubbed his nose again. "That's all of it, I guess. I'll be back when, Frank?"

"Day after tomorrow," said Frank LaWall. "I want to

be sure that Dirty Henry has gone to town. Keep your eyes peeled and if anything breaks—something we can use to our advantage—let me know, Hans."

"I'll do that," agreed Hans Sexton.

"Ride light," murmured Frank LaWall. Sexton got up and went away, and soon they heard his horse moving out there in the night. They hunkered and each had his thoughts. Finally Dusty Jacobson got to his feet. "Time for the sougans," he said. *"Buenas noches, hombres."* He went into the dark. Soon the door to the bunkhouse opened and light came out and was cut off as the door closed. A horse snorted and stomped in a corral and a cow bawled off across the hills.

LaWall said, "Time for bed, Jib."

"A little more of the night for me," said Jib Hobson. "I like the night, Frank. It makes a man feel his right size."

LaWall spoke carefully. "Night's too big for a man, Jib. A man wants somethin' his size, somethin' he can see and fight. A man's in the dark a long time after he closes his eyes. There'll be a day when all of us get plenty of sleep. While we're here, play the game hard...."

"Your version," said Jib Hobson; "not mine."

"We disagree on a lot of things." LaWall moved toward the house and went inside. Jib Hobson sat there and listened to the door close. He thought of Hans Sexton, riding back to the dirt camp.

He sat there for an hour. Then finally, with the chill in the air, he got up and went into the dark bunkhouse. Men were snoring and stirring in their sleep, and he got the smell of warm bodies in a close place. He climbed into his bunk and opened the window at his head. The air was calm and sharp and he pulled it into him. From here he could see the Milky Way, a giant belt studded with distant diamonds. He went to sleep finally, thinking of Janice Braden....

CHAPTER 6

WHEN SIN BRADEN pulled the team in, Dondo came from the brush, a smile on his wrinkled face. He said to Buck and Tortilla Joe, "How," and added: "Dondo glad to see you again."

Sin Braden slapped Dondo's back. "You little redskinned rascal," she said good-naturedly.

Another Ilak, small as Dondo, came from the brush. "This is my brother, Pone," introduced Dondo. "He see big mans—LaWall an' Hobson an' Jacobson—ride to N Bar S ranch."

"They all there now," said Pone.

"Where's the rest of your tribe?" asked Buck.

"They leave, like I tell you."

Buck smiled. "You misunderstand me. I mean your women."

"They over hill. Camped there. Ogo, Pipo an' Nono. Ogo my wife, Pipo an' Nono daughters."

"Yeah, they're all here," said Sin Braden. She put her arm around Dondo and hugged him. He smiled widely and chuckled.

"She my girl," he said.

Tortilla Joe untied their saddle-horses while Buck and Dondo and Pone unhooked the team. Dirt men were lying on blankets in front of their tents and a few of them were shooting craps on the table in the cook tent. A man came over to take the team. Sin introduced him to Buck.

"Hans Sexton, Buck. One of my best dirt men."

Sexton shook hands. "You're new here, huh?"

"Colonel Henry S. Braden sent him an' Tortilla Joe to side us," said Sin Braden. "Them an' the colonel fit through the war together."

Buck noticed that Sexton glanced at his gun and that of Tortilla before the dirt man led the team away. A long man, heavy and solid, swaggered up. He looked like an ape, Buck decided. He had long arms and his massive face was covered with a black beard. Sin Braden introduced him as Jens Jones.

"Our dirt boss," she finished. "Used to ramrod gangs down on the levees in Alabama and Mississippi. Knows dirt and knows how to handle it, Buck."

Buck shook hands. Jones had a grip like a vise. Buck had to grit his teeth. "You do that to everybody?" he asked.

Jones' grip relaxed instantly. "I'm sorry," he said. "I just forget sometimes, I guess." White teeth showed behind his beard.

Buck liked the fellow. He made a mental note then and there: if he ever had any trouble with Jens Jones, he would be sure to keep the man at a distance. For if a man ever got locked in the dirt-boss' arms, he would crush him.

He and Tortilla met the rest of the camp. Some of the fresno men were farmers: Ralph Knox, Thad Johnson, Bill Dighton and Max Ayers. Dirty Henry Smutton got up and shook hands. Buck decided he was the dirtiest man he had ever seen. Cockleburrs hung to his scraggly beard and his clothes were held together by wire and staples. His hand was thick with dirt that looked like it had been there for years.

"He only uses water to drink," said Sin Braden. "And he'd drink little of that, if there was a case of hootch around."

"I guess I'll take a barrel of whiskey into camp," said Dirty Henry Smutton, grinning.

"And I'll skin you alive," gritted Sin Braden. "No whiskey in this camp, Dirty Henry, if you value your life."

Dondo held his nose. "Him stink."

Dirty Henry made a grab for the pygmy Ilak. Dondo nimbly stepped out of reach. "You couldn't catch dead deer in snowbank," said Dondo. "You hate to hear truth, huh?"

"Can that, Dondo!" snapped Sin Braden.

Janice Braden had gone to her tent. Sin showed Tortilla Joe and Buck their tent and they threw their warbags inside. The cook hollered, "Come an' get it, you late comers!" and then added some cursing. According to him, each night saw him cooking later and later, and he'd walk off pronto if he had to do the same tomorrow night.

"He's said that all summer," said Sin.

"A pot rassler's loco," grunted Tortilla Joe. "If he wasn't, he wouldn't be a pot rassler, huh?"

The meal was good. Boiled antelope steak and sweet potatoes, the latter raised by a farmer. Already a chill was in the evening air. Tortilla Joe warmed up a *tortilla* on the big cookstove. He sipped his coffee noisily.

"I am ready to heet the hay," he said.

Buck spoke to Janice. "Tonight this camp will be cursed with some outrageous snoring. Anybody in hearing distance of Tortilla's bed can hear him."

Janice said, "You both sleep in the same tent."

"I got automatic ear-drums," stated Buck. "I can shut off my ears when I want to. Besides that, I used to work in a boiler factory."

"Humph . . ." snorted Sin Braden.

The meal completed, they went outside. Buck and Tortilla went to their tent. Tortilla rolled out his sougans, pulled off his boots, hung up his hat and went to bed. He lay on his side, almost completely dressed, his head on one arm. Buck saw that the evening concert was soon to start. He walked outside and circled the camp. Dondo came out of the rosebushes.

"You walk around, huh?"

Buck said, "Restless."

"Me an' Pone on guard. Some of the farmers go home, do chores. Some have children, see. Me, Pone guard."

Buck and the small Apache sat among the rocks. The stars came out and the wind died down. Both were silent. Buck was glad that his companion did not press him into conversation. He was tired. Events and circumstances had happened quickly in the last few hours. He and Tortilla Joe had ridden into the valley to see Sin Braden, who turned out to be an old friend, Cattle Annie.

He looked toward the N Bar S. He could see the spread's lights: they twinkled in space. They were innocent looking, he decided. But in those buildings, behind those lights, were rough, tough men. Man was a fool for fighting, he thought. The land would be here when the last man was gone. Then what was the use of fighting over it?

This was but one of his thoughts. He had dwelt mentally before on man's frailties, short-comings and virtues.

These he had discussed around campfires, on the trail. He had no love for farmers. They broke up the land that cattle and buffalo used to graze on. They were running the cowman and the cowpuncher out of existence. But the cattle had brought about the virtual extinction of the buffalo. And the cattle, and their owners, would have to give way to farmers.

This was one of the rigid rules of life. Either you change with the time or you fall back into time and lose your contact with reality. The war had taught him that; the lesson had been carefully learned. He closed his eyes and leaned back. Lassitude flowed into him and possessed him. He awoke when Dondo poked him in the ribs.

"Rider come, *Senor* Buck."

Buck came awake quickly. He had his hand on his gun, then he drew it back. Pone came out of the brush. He came quietly and he settled beside his brother. "Hans Sexton," he said. "He ride in."

Sexton rode into camp. "Prob'ly been to his farm," murmured Buck. "He has one, hasn't he?"

Dondo said, "I guess so."

Sexton unsaddled his horse and tied him to the long feed rack. He fed him some bluestem hay and went to his tent. Buck got to his feet slowly. "I better get to bed," he said. "When do other guards relieve you two?"

"Never," grunted Pone.

Buck studied the swarthy pygmy. "Explain yourself."

Pone looked at Dondo. "You talk better'n me. Tell Buck?"

Dondo asked, "You want to hear, Buck?"

"If you care to tell me, yes."

Dondo spoke. "We camp by river. Mad River. You hear it, don't you? They call it mad. No, not mad. Good river, if you know him. He feed Apache, fish. He furnish baskets, willows. You listen, white man?"

"Yes."

"Ilak wander tribe. Leave real Apaches. Hit out for themselves. We come to Mad River. Like river, settle there. Here a year, Me, Pone, family. Other Ilaks, too. We good people."

Pone nodded. Buck listened.

"LaWall lose cow, so he say. He accuse us. We no have. We no kill. He come at night——"

"Jacobson, too," said Pone.

Dondo spoke huskily. "They kill. We get away—five of us. That was two months ago. What good law? Ilaks wander tribe. Law does not like. Ilaks make own law. Not enough to fight LaWall. Go to Sin Braden. Later——"

Buck nodded, silent.

Pone sighed heavily. Dondo held his head in his hands. His muscular body trembled. Finally he looked up. "Now you know, Buck."

Buck murmured, "Thanks, friend."

The intensity of the man's tone had shaken him. In it he read a pent-up hatred, an undying hatred.

"Ilak, never sleep," said Pone.

Buck got to his feet and said, "See you come mornin'." He went to his tent. Hans Sexton spoke from the shadows. "You're up late, McKee."

"Couldn't sleep," said Buck. "How come you're awake?"

"Been to my homestead, just got back. Didn't you see me ride in?"

Buck said, "Was back on the hill, I guess." Tortilla Joe was snoring loudly. Buck lighted a match and looked at his Mexican partner. Tortilla lay on his back, his mouth wide open. His lips fluttered as he inhaled and exhaled, his huge chest rising under his blanket.

The match burned down. Buck lay under his blankets. The noise was too loud. That, coupled with his thoughts, made no sleep for him. He stood it for an hour, anyway. A number of times he almost went to sleep but, at these periods, Tortilla Joe rolled over, snoring right into his ear. Finally Buck got up. He lighted another match, eyes grave.

"Damned steam calliope," he mumbled.

He saw Tortilla Joe's bag of *tortillas*. Holding the match in one hand, he got out a *tortilla*. He jammed it hard into his partner's open mouth, then rolled into his sougans hurriedly, the match extinguished.

Tortilla Joe woke up gasping. He said, *"Sangre de Dios, que esta?"* and in English, "What ees thees theeng?" He lighted a match and looked at the *tortilla*. Buck was watching through lidded eyes, leaving just a crack of space to see through. Tortilla Joe glared at him.

"You do thees to me, Buck?"

Buck mumbled, feigning sleep.

Tortilla Joe shook him. "I say—you do thees theeng to me, *verdad?*"

Buck opened his eyes. "Go to sleep, you fool," he growled. "Who did what to you——" He rolled over, his back to his partner. The tent went dark as Tortilla Joe's match went out.

He heard the Mexican grunt, "Now who put thees in my mouth?" There was a moment's silence. Then he heard his partner start eating the *tortilla*. Tortilla Joe smacked his lips noisily, sucked through his teeth, mumbled as he chewed.

"That Peta Gomez, she ees the wonder at the *tortilla,* no? Why deed not I marry her, huh?"

Buck did not answer.

Tortilla Joe fell silent, chewing on his *tortilla*. Again his lips smacked: he sucked and chewed. Buck wondered which was worse: his snoring or his eating. But he never got to a conclusion. Sleep took him too quickly.

CHAPTER 7

BUCK AND TORTILLA were up with the sun. For already the camp was astir. The cook was singing, high and off-key. In between words of the song he interjected cuss words. Buck decided that the man swore because he was happy.

Men were grumbling and splashing as they washed in the tin basins. They filed into the tent, took seats on the long benches, and ate breakfast. There was no loafing after the meal. With cigarettes lighted, they went to the corral, got their teams, harnessed the horses.

There were no skittish broncs, no rearing or kicking. The horses had labored hard on fresnos and scrapers and dirt-wagons and all the orneriness had left them. Buck helped a lanky kid hitch his four horses to a fresno. Jens Jones came up, his long arms swinging.

"You an' Tortilla Joe goin' do some work, Buck."

"I'll take a turn at a fresno for a while," said Buck.

"But I don't know about Tortilla Joe. If you get any work out of him, you're doin' somethin' that nobody else has been able to do as yet."

"Gracias," Tortilla Joe grinned widely. "I drive a dirt-wagon, huh?"

The kid was glad to be relieved of fresno duty. He was assigned to a dirt-wagon. Hans Sexton acted as dump boss on the fill. Tugs rattled and wagon wheels creaked. The day had begun.

"Move that sod," hollered Jens Jones. "Time to rattle your tug chains, you dirt-monkeys! Put them work-broncs against them collars an' keep them there!"

They were working above the dam. They were digging dirt out of the hill there and moving it down into the dam's fill. This way, the capacity of the dam would be enlarged; the dirt would be dug out in back of it. Already the ploughs were cutting into the gravel and sod to loosen it for the fresnos.

After the sod had been busted loose, the fresnos came. Buck lay down on the handle, holding the blade in the ground. A man had to watch what he was doing. For, if the blade caught on a rock unexpectedly, the handle would fly up. If this occurred, the driver would lose his load.

Behind him were strung out the other fresno men with their four horses ahead, making them pull hard as he loaded his fresno. With the bucket full, the pulling was easier. He started toward the dump.

The dump, made of heavy logs, was set high enough for a team and dirt-wagon to pass under. Drivers stopped their wagons under the hole and, when the fresnos passed over them, the loads were dumped down the hole into the wagons. When a wagon was full, the driver drove out on the fill, and, at Jens Jones' order, dumped his load by releasing the bottom of his wagon, letting the dirt fall down on the dam.

The work was slow, hard and tedious for the fresno operators. They plodded along behind their labouring horses. But it was easier for the wagon-men. All they did was ride their seats, stop their wagons on the right spot under the dump, and then dump them at Jens Jones' orders.

A pall of dust hung over the operations. The early

morning chill departed and the heat of forenoon started creeping in. Sweat formed under the collars and breeching straps of the horses. Methodically they plodded along. The husky curses of the drivers hung on the hot atmosphere.

Janice Braden was patching a hole in a tent. She had a bottle of some glue of some sort and she was seated on a rock, sewing the patch on after she had stuck it on the canvas with glue. She lifted her hand to Buck. Sin Braden was standing by Jens Jones, watching the fill grow. Tortilla Joe came up with his wagon. Jones showed him where to drop his dirt.

The Mexican kicked the release lever and the split-bottom of his wagon broke open, depositing the gravel and sod on the dam. Sin Braden looked up at him and grinned. "What's on your so-called mind, you fat rascal?"

Tortilla Joe's broad face was caked with dust and sweat. His broad grin cracked the heavy coat of dust. "Thees job, she ees good for a man that has no job, maybe, an' has to work, no? But for me—me, I like the saddle too *mucho*."

"Born to the leather," said Sin, "an prob'ly born to be hung. How's Buck holdin' up?"

Tortilla Joe glanced at his partner. Buck was leaning on his fresno-handle, holding the blade in the earth. "He ees a cowboy on foots," said the Mexican. "An' no cowboy should be on his boots, no?"

"Yes," corrected Sin Braden. "Do him good. He can realize how lucky he is to be a horseman, not a sheepherder."

Tortilla Joe snapped his off-horse across the rump. He went back for another load. Hans Sexton was boss on the dump. He rubbed his crooked nose and grunted something. Tortilla Joe looked at his nose.

"What happen to your nose, huh?"

"Apache war-axe," said Sexton. "I ducked a little too slow, I reckon. Over in the battle of Chimney Rocks, over twenty years ago. Split my snozzle wide open and we sewed it with saddle-whang. Never did appreciate our work, 'cause it grew on crooked."

"An' the Apache?"

"He never cut another white man," said Sexton. "Okay,

Joe, your load is full. Drag her out an' put her on the dam, cowhand."

Buck was getting tired. A saddleman, he had walked little; now, still in high-heel boots, he was petering out. Not that he would admit it. Nevertheless, he was glad when Jens Jones finally hollered, "Noon, boys. Unhook and feed your horses an' come a-runnin' to the slop trough!"

Buck's feet were sore. He had not seen Dondo or Pone all morning. After eating, he climbed the hill. Dondo was still seated among the rocks, rifle beside him. He looked like he had not stirred since Buck had seen him the night before. He settled down beside the pygmy Apache.

"How, Dondo."

"How, Buck."

"Where's Pone?"

Buck settled back into the shade. He sat down and rested. "You ride fresno," said Dondo suddenly. "I see you. You rest now, need it."

Buck nodded.

"Hard work. You saddle-boy. Saddle-boy no good on foot. You stay with horse. Need man on horse, maybe. I talk with Sin. She say all right to tell you."

"Tell me what?"

"About Sexton. Hans Sexton. Him spy for LaWall. Him draw LaWall money. We know. Jib Hobson tell us."

"What're you talkin' about? Sexton works for Sin Braden; Jib Hobson works for LaWall."

Dondo's seamed face showed a smile. "Sure, we know. But Jib jus' work for us—him is spy. Our spy."

Buck understood then. "Right tough job," he murmured. "If'n LaWall fin's out, he'll cut young Jib's brisket to small hunks with a dull butcher knife. So Sexton is a spy in our camp, huh?"

"That's where he was last night," said Dondo. "He over to N Bar S, talk with LaWall. Ogo follow him part way. On foot. She smart woman. Sin Braden smart woman, too. Me, I like Sin." He chuckled. "She my girl, huh?"

Buck scowled. Sin Braden came up the hill. She settled down and pulled a straw out of a clump of dried grass and started picking her teeth. "Reckon this savage has tol' you the news, huh, Buck?"

Buck said, "He sure has, Sin."

Sin scowled and picked harder. "No use bracin' Hans Sexton," she finally said. "As long as we have Jib Hobson in their camp, Sexton can't be very dangerous to us. But I am sort of worried about Jib. You see, him an' Janice are engaged, and if Jib got killed off——"

"LaWall or Jacobson find out he's a spy," said Buck, "an' they'll be apt to kill him. Better not let the word spread around 'cause if Sexton finds out——" He drew his forefinger suggestively across his throat.

"Just tell Tortilla, nobody else," said Sin.

Buck got to his feet. Dirt-men were stirring down below them, going to their horses to hook them for the second half of the day. "I'm stiff," he mumbled. "These ol' bones aren't used to such hard labour."

Sin spat out the straw. "No dirt-work this afternoon for you an' Tortilla Joe, Buck. Saddle your broncs an' me an' you an' Janice will do some look-seein' around the other dams we've built. You'll want to get the lay of the land in your mind, too; it might come in handy some dark night."

"Uh-huh," said Buck.

Janice rode a sorrel gelding with a buckskin mane and tail. She was a pretty girl on a pretty horse, Buck decided. Outside of that, she didn't affect him much. A woman was a woman, when he was concerned.

He could take them or leave them. It was different with Tortilla Joe: he had a sweetheart wherever he stopped any length of time. But Buck was watchful enough to notice that his partner always picked a woman who could cook good *tortillas* and knew how to properly season *frijoles* with *chili* peppers. The extent and intensity of Tortilla Joe's love was determined by the lady's cooking ability.

"We ride, no?" asked Tortilla Joe, wide face beaming. "Thees job on horseback ees better than on a wagon seat, Buck. Surely I was never meant to be a farmer."

The morning rest, coupled with plenty of bluestem and two messes of oats, had put life back into their wiry cowponies. Sin Braden rode heavily on an iron-grey, a big horse of about fifteen hundred. She held the reins in a sun-tanned fist, her heavy face determined.

"Come on, Tortilla," said Sin Braden huskily. "Rattle your rowels, you cowdog. We got ridin' to do."

Pone squatted in the buckbrush at the base of the hill. Sin Braden talked to him in sign language. Pone nodded his head. Buck had read her rapidly-moving hands: *We ride out, Pone. We come back at dusk.* Pone went back into the rosebushes. The underbrush rippled, settled. A rider could never see the short Apache there with his rifle and his long knife.

"Good guards," grunted Sin.

The afternoon sun was intensely hot so they did not ride fast. They headed for Mad River, riding through herds of N Bar S cattle. Here on the lower lands the cattle were not so wild; they were tame compared to those in the hills. Sin showed them the crossings on Mad River. Below them the water boiled and sang, heading for the Gulf of Lower California.

There were a number of fenced lanes in the section of the valley. Cowboys and homesteaders alike had settled here; the cowpunchers for their boss, LaWall; the homesteaders, to build their homes here. According to law, some improvement had to be done on the land other than the construction of buildings—some land had to be ploughed and sowed into crop.

Because irrigation water had not been available here, the crops had sprouted and grown a few inches, then died and burned under the hot sun. But when water came, this would be a good farming land. Buck took note of this and Tortilla Joe summed up the whole situation with a few well-chosen words.

"Weeth plenty of waters, the crops they weel grow good here, no? Thees weel be a green farm land with plenty of homes an' good crops an' children." He lifted his wide shoulders and let them fall. "But for me, I cannot see eet, Buck. When that happens, people settle down—they do not even pack the guns. Then I weel be in *Mejico*, no, below the border where there ees the desert and the cattles."

"An' me with you," said Buck.

"Here's Mud Crick dam," said Sin Braden.

The earth-filled dam lay in a coulee below them. It was complete with rock-lined spillways and with both faces of the dam lined with boulders and gravel. This was to keep erosion from affecting the dirt. A hard rain could wash the face of the dam down were it not lined with rock.

Behind it lay a broad, flat-bottomed coulee. Springs back against the hills had built a small reservoir behind the dam. Buck could see the top of a yucca lily out in the water: that meant it was as deep as a man is tall. Already quite a bit of water had been stored.

Buck rode down-slope and looked at the base of the dam. He had expected seepage to come through but there was none. Sin Braden then explained that this soil had a high adobe content and, when water hit, it had a tendency to set, much as concrete did. Buck nodded slowly. . . .

"That dam'll be there for a long time," he allowed.

They rode to other dams: they had various names—Barr, Skunk, Wildcat, Johnson, Timber. During the few months she had been in the basin, Sin Braden and her men had done a lot of work. Each dam had guards around it. They were guarded night and day, according to Sin, who stressed the fact that, as long as Frank LaWall and his cattle were in the basin, the dams would continue to be guarded.

They were riding down a coulee when a man came out of the brush ahead. Buck dropped his hand to his gun and the rider held up his right hand, palm spread out. He was strongly familiar to him. And Janice's gasped, "Why, that's Jib!" brought his hand up empty.

Jib Hobson said, "Hello, Janice," and kissed her. Buck saw that the girl's eyes were sparkling. Then Jib talked in a low, fast tone of voice. He told them that LaWall planned to hit Dirty Henry Smutton's farm and burn the buildings.

"When?" asked Buck.

"Tomorrow night. Sexton knows about it, Buck. He was in on the pow-wow. I'll ride with LaWall an' Jacobson, of course."

Janice's pretty face showed concern. "You be careful, Jib. There might be some shooting and in the dark——"

Jib patted her hand. "Now don't you worry, honey. One thing is certain—we have to have a spy in the N Bar S camp. Otherwise we'll never know what LaWall's plottin'. Sure glad you an' Tortilla come to side us, Buck."

"You watch your trail," said Buck grimly. "You're ridin' on a crumblin' ledge, young feller, an' it might give way any time under your weight."

Jib smiled. Buck liked the ways of this brainy, good-looking kid. "I better be scootin' back to the camp, Buck. I'm out ridin' bog holes, accordin' to what I tol' the boss. You folks ride right down the gully. I'll sneak along an' come up the other way an' nobody'll know we met."

He rode away.

Buck and his party rode on. They were for the most part silent. A mile from camp, Sin Braden spoke. "What plan do you say, Buck?"

Buck shoved back his Tom Watson Stetson and scratched his head slowly. "Only one thing to do, Sin. Get a handful of men an' surround Dirty Henry's cabin. Then, when they come they'll walk into our trap. We'll be on the legal side—they came to rob and burn and we'll be fightin' to pertect Dirty Henry's property."

"Can the legality of it," growled Sin. "By the time Nappy Hale got on a trail, the trail'll be so ol' the wind'll have swept the tracks away. An' if we get in deep, Colonel Henry S. Braden'll get us out—he's got plenty of influence at Tucson an' Phoenix."

"Tomorrow night, huh?" mumbled Tortilla Joe.

CHAPTER 8

WHEN DUSK finally came, Frank LaWall went to the horse corral. The *mozo* had already saddled three horses —black horses, all of them. Night broncs. War Chief was in bed and Feather Eagle had been washing the dishes, therefore neither knew Frank LaWall had left the house, what with the kitchen on the other side of the big structure.

Jib Hobson and Dusty Jacobson were hunkered beside the barn. They got to their feet when LaWall came to the corral and went toward him, the big Jacobson slightly ahead of the thin young puncher.

46

Jacobson said, "There'll be kerosene out at Dirty Henry's, Frank. I saw him buy a five-gallon can the other day in town."

"I got a can cached down the trail," growled LaWall. He looked at the old *mozo* who stood beside the corral gate. "We're riding over on the south prairie, *viejo*. Somebody over there's been snippin' our drift fence some night an' we aim to run the fellow down to earth. If anybody asks for us, you don't know nothin', *sabe?*"

The old *mozo* had seen a lot of life. He nodded and said, "I see nothin', *senor*." He opened the gate and they rode out. Frank LaWall took the lead, riding deep in saddle; he was morose, and silent. Dusty Jacobson fell beside his boss and Jib Hobson rode to one side. They packed saddle-carbines and each had a gunny-sack tied over his saddle-skirts with a box of rifle and a box of .45 cartridges in each sack.

"No need to hurry," said Dusty Jacobson slowly. "We don't want to get over there until it's dark."

"Quite a ride," muttered Frank LaWall.

Jib Hobson was silent. He watched the night gather: they rode into it, they broke it apart. He did not like the role he was playing—because of him men might die. But he satisfied himself by saying his role was essential to peace on this valley. He himself had taken up a homestead. LaWall figured he had taken it for him to purchase later, but LaWall was mistaken. He would marry Janice and settle on his homestead. He would get additional land on a grazing entry and run cattle back in the hills; not many head, but enough to trail out a few each fall and to have a beef or two to hang in the cooler. And to do this, Frank LaWall would have to be eliminated. That thought was grim, but it had to be. For if Frank LaWall could not read the handwriting left by progress, then he would have to be shoved aside to let progress continue.

LaWall had acted hurriedly, placing punchers on homesteads; but the Basin was too huge; he and his men could not homestead all of it. Now, heading for Dirty Henry Smutton's, he knew he was making a big move, a move that might backfire, or a move that might go over—and scare settlers out of Mad River valley.

He had weighed the thing in his mind for sometime.

This move was drastic and he fully appreciated its danger. Had the time been twenty years before, there would have been no menace in it. Then, cattlemen were strong—they controlled the territorial legislature; they had ridden on tall horses. But now, irrigation was creeping into Arizona, coming across the mountains, the deserts. And the influence of the cattlemen had deteriorated much in the last two decades.

He drew in. "The kerosene can," he said; "it's in the brush."

Dusty Jacobson stepped down. He found the gallon can and shook it. There was no sound of splashing; the can was full. "Should be enough, Frank," he murmured. He tied the can to the rope-strap on his fork and climbed up again and they rode on. Jacobson was scowling in the darkness.

He had come to Mad River some twenty years before, a stripling in his twenties. Already a top hand, he had signed on as bronc-stomper for the N Bar S, breaking saddle-stock to ride for cowpunchers. From there, he had gone up to straw-boss, and finally Frank LaWall had made him his foreman. He, too, was aware of this growing danger, this piled-up menace.

But his roots were deep into this land. He and Frank LaWall had ridden many trails together, rodded roundup wagons, roped as a team during calf roundup. Between them was a deep friendship—they were two big men, and each appreciated the strength of the other.

They came to a ridge. Below them lay the valley and on it were the lights marking the homes of the settlers. Frank LaWall said, "Wait a minute, men," and sat silent, looking at this land and wondering if he would lose it. His face graven and inscrutable, wrapped in darkness, he sat his leather and looked at the lamplights. His eyes ran across the flatness to Dirty Henry Smutton's house on the flat above the gorge of Mad River.

No lights there, he thought.

The wind was sighing through the pine trees. He shifted a little, putting his weight on his other stirrup, and he looked to the north. Two lights glowed and he marked their location, and he looked at Dusty Jacobson.

"Bill Dighton isn't home," said LaWall. "His outfit is dark. It's a long ride over to Dirty Henry's cabin. . . ."

Jacobson nodded.

LaWall looked at Jib Hobson. "Bill Dighton's a bachelor, ain't he? He ain't got no kin on his spread, has he?"

"I don't know . . . for sure."

Dusty Jacobson jerked his head around sharply and looked at Jib Hobson. "What the hell's wrong with your memory, Jib? Of course, Dighton's a bach—he ain't got no kin here. I thought you knew that."

"I don't give a damn about these pun'kin rollers," said Jib Hobson.

LaWall touched his horse. "No use ridin' all the way to Dirty Henry's," he said stoutly. "We'll hit Bill Dighton's spread. That way, if anything does go haywire, we can pull back into the hills, an' nobody could cut us off—like they could if we rode clean across the Basin to Dirty Henry's."

Jacobson grunted, swung in behind his boss. Behind him came Jib Hobson. They rode down the slope, their broncs braced against gravity. Hobson thought; *Buck McKee, Tortilla Joe and their bunch are waiting . . . at Dirty Henry's. But we hit Bill Dighton's, instead.* He knew that Dighton was with the dirt-crew. Perhaps he had ridden home to do chores, but he had evidently ridden back to the dirt-camp . . . if he had ever ridden home that evening. Hobson tried to remember what he had heard about Bill Dighton: Did the man have any chickens, cows, or any other farm animals that would require attention each morning and evening? Had he come home to tend to them and did he sleep now in his cabin?

Jib Hobson looked at the dark building ahead of them. No, Dighton was not home, it was too early to go to sleep—the place must be deserted. He hoped so. He knew that if Dighton were home, there would be shooting. Not that he was afraid to be involved in a gun ruckus. He'd be willing to take a chance against a bullet—he had done so many times . . . But he hated to see a man shot down in his own house and then devoured by its flames.

Fate and circumstance had kicked back against him, throwing his plans out of proportion. There was nothing he could do now—all he could do was play the hand through, and hope the cards fell right.

They reached the level land, circled the rim of the foothills, moving ahead at a running-walk. Twenty minutes later, they sat in the high brush and looked at the dark buildings ahead. Dighton had a log two-room house, a small barn also built of pine logs, and they could see a windlass ahead, for the man was digging a well. Frank LaWall smiled.

"Don't fall down that well, any of you."

Dusty Jacobson said, "You two stay here, an' I'll scout aroun'." The night seemed to reach out and grab him. They heard his boots move off and then there was only the sound of the wind.

Jib Hobson listened for the bark of a dog, thinking perhaps Bill Dighton had a cur. But none came and the youth settled back. They waited about ten minutes, with Frank LaWall hunkered into a big ball, and with Jib Hobson resting against a boulder. Their horses stood with dragging reins.

Suddenly Jacobson was back. "Nobody home," he said. "No dog, no chickens. Got a cow out in a night-pasture. The thing is clear and open, Frank, an' the outfit is as good as ashes."

"That's good," said Frank LaWall. "Sure didn't want to have to kill somebody, Dusty. This should scare some of these settlers out of the Basin. If it don't we'll take sterner measures. But we better try this an' then make tracks out fast and few. You got the kerosene, Hobson?"

"I got it."

"Give it to me," said Jacobson.

The job didn't take long. A stack of dried hay—mostly buckbrush and wild grass—stood behind the barn. They soaked the base of it and the house and the barn and three matches did it. Jib Hobson fired the haystack. He watched the flame catch, watched it spread; he went to his horse.

He stood there, one hand on his saddle, and watched the house and the barn come into flame. Dusty Jacobson came running, carrying the empty kerosene can. He grabbed his reins and went up. He said, "Where the hell is Frank?"

"Here he comes."

Frank LaWall gritted, "Get out of here, Hobson," and he hit leather. Jib Hobson was up by this time and they rode off, galloping north against the night. They would circle, cutting around an arc; then they would come in on the N Bar S. That way, if anybody tried to trail them, they would lose their tracks on the gravel and the rough hills.

Dusty Jacobson took the lead, braced against his fork. Hobson came behind him, thinking of this night and its misdeeds, and behind the slim rider came big Frank LaWall, chuckling to himself. They rode this way for about two miles, then they reached the higher rim.

Frank LaWall said, "Wait a minute," and they turned their horses. "Rest our broncs a bit."

"Makes a nice fire," he admitted.

Jib Hobson grunted, "Could roast a nice piece of venison in that." He said it not because he wanted to, but because he thought the words were proper.

But Frank LaWall was thinking ahead. "They'll see the flame an' ride over from the dirt camp. Of course, they'll suspect us of settin' it, but they can't prove nothin'. Might do some good, though. Let's hope so."

"If it doesn't?" asked Dusty Jacobson.

Frank LaWall was silent for ten seconds. Then he said, "Let's ride for home," and he turned his horse, the question unanswered.

CHAPTER 9

THAT EVENING, Buck McKee had watched Hans Sexton closely, yet the man had made no move to sneak away. Buck had figured maybe he would go to the N Bar S and ride with Frank LaWall and Dusty Jacobson and Jib Hobson against Dirty Henry Smutton's property. But Hans Sexton went to bed early. Shortly after sundown, he was snoring between his blankets.

"Ogo watch him," said Dondo.

The wrinkled, ageless squaw had grinned toothlessly at Buck. "I cut his throat some day," she said.

Buck smiled. "Not now, Ogo. Postpone it a while."

She said, "I watch him close."

Buck and Tortilla Joe and Jens had ridden off. Down

the trail, they met Sin Braden, sitting her horse beside a sandstone. Buck scowled and said, "There might be trouble, Sin. You'd better stay home."

"I can handle it as good as you," declared Sin. "I snuck away from Janice; she wanted to come. Well, let's ride."

They were all armed. Each rider carried a saddle-carbine and had his belt filled with shot-gun cartridges. Even Sin packed a rifle—a Winchester .25-35, a deadly gun even at a distance. She had strapped a .45 around her enormous girth. A sloppy old hat was perched on her rolled-up hair, a long hairpin jammed through its crown. She wore a checkered flannel shirt and levis that were crammed into worn boots. She sat solidly in her saddle.

Buck saw that she meant business. And when she meant business, woe to any man or woman that stood in her way. He had seen her bounce drunks in her saloon, when she was known as Cattle Annie. Many times she had picked up a small man and bodily thrown him outside of her establishment.

Tortilla Joe munched at a *tortilla*. Jens Jones's big frame was jammed between the fork and cantle of his Monkey Ward saddle. The dirt-boss was growling under his breath. He was tired and sleepy but he had not wanted to miss the fun, as he called it. Buck had mentally disagreed with him on the word *fun:* there might be some gunplay when they surprised the N Bar S hands.

It was dark when they reached Dirty Henry's cabin. The buildings lay along the base of a small hill that was spotted with *chamiso* and *yucca* and buckbrush. The outline of the buildings were apparent in the night.

They left their horses in the brush above Mad River. The river boiled and sang, rolling downward over rocks. They went toward the cabin, moving through the buckbrush. A wood rat scurried away from them and Sin Braden stopped suddenly. "What was that?"

Tortilla Joe chuckled. "A reever rat, Seen. You are a big girl, now, too; a darned beeg girl, huh?" His chuckle grew stronger.

Sin was angry. "You're gettin' kinda big yourself, Joe; especially out toward the front, not up. You're gettin' to pack aroun' quite an extension there."

"That ees because of the *tortillas*."

The buckbrush was thick in spots and the night was dark; travelling through it was no easy chore. Jens Jones walked right into a catclaw that grew along a tree, and the sharp throngs hit his face, bringing a little blood. Buck heard him curse under his breath.

Each carried his rifle. Sin Braden used hers as a bar to brush the rosebushes aside, carrying it out in front of her. They came to the back of Dirty Henry's cabin and they stood there and looked at the buildings. Buck had already drawn up a plan of procedure but he again issued his orders.

"Tortilla Joe an' Sin, you two take the east side of the outfit, over along the base of that hill. Spread out and be sure you don't let them get the barn or haystacks on fire. Call them to surrender, an' if'n they don't give up —then you'll have to persuade them with lead, I reckon."

Sin Braden patted her rifle barrel. "A good persuader," she said drily.

"Me an' Jens Jones'll take the west side. We'll be there on guard. Now mind, if you do shoot, be careful of the fellow opposite you, even though he is hid in brush. There might be an outside chance of hittin' him. But, if it does come to shootin', we'll be shootin' down, so there is less danger that way. All right, everything clear?"

"She ees clear, *Senor* Buck." Tortilla Joe crossed himself reverently. "Me, I hope no shootin' she ees to be done —I do not like to hear the bullets seeng in the air. Eet makes me nervous, no?"

"No," said Buck.

Tortilla Joe had taken the crystal off his dollar watch. Now his stubby fingers were feeling the dial. Finally he said, "I cannot make out what time it is, Buck. What luck have you?" He handed Buck his Ingersoll.

Buck felt of the hands in the dark. Finally he said, "Feels like the minute hand is on about two an' the hour hand is on nine. Ten after nine, I'd say."

"They'll hit aroun' midnight, I'd say," put in Jens Jones.

"We can't take any chances on bein' caught flat-footed." Buck's voice was calm. "We better get into positions."

With Jens Jones following, Buck led the way. He stationed the dirt-boss beside a giant cottonwood and he went ahead, squatting beside a dwarf oak. Save for occasional nocturnal sounds, the night was still. The air was getting snappy and the thermometer would get lower as the night progressed.

Settled on his spurs, Buck thought of many things. He had, in his short lifetime, seen quite a bit of bloodshed and strife, and he hoped that this affair would not end as had some of the others. He debated about the best procedure to squelch Frank LaWall and Dusty Jacobson. Would it be better to let LaWall do the action, bring about the trouble, and then have himself and Tortilla Joe settle it? Or would it be better to move out and front LaWall, driving him to a showdown?

Running over the two plans, Buck found little difference in them. One phrase stood out prominently in the first plan. Perhaps, after bucking them a few times, LaWall would get wise, call it quits, and console himself with the thought of having farmers on his range?

That would mean one thing: LaWall would have to cut down on the size of his N Bar S herd, and Buck had a hunch the cowman would not want to do that. Though, from what Buck had heard, this could be accomplished without losing any income from cattle. For, with less range to graze on, some cattlemen had taken to breeding better cattle—cattle with more beef on them and cattle that were easier to handle.

Buck ran all this through his mind, hoping that LaWall would take this out, thereby discarding this threatened range war. But he knew he would be wrong. LaWall was of the old-school cowmen; he had, by sweat and hard work, built up the N Bar S, stocking Mad River Basin with his cattle. Now he would not lose that range, even though farmers were settling legally on land he had run cattle over. He had a strong, strange pride; Buck thought *only a bullet could change it.*

He had seen it before.

Buck shifted positions, debating about this part of man's make-up. Somewhere an owl was hooting, back yonder on the ridge. A wood rat ran across the trail ahead of him. The rodent stopped, and Buck saw his small shiny eyes. He stood tense and then he scurried away, moving out of sight and hearing.

Buck moved over to Jens Jones. He said, "I'm going across an' see Tortilla, Jens." The big man nodded and Buck moved away. When he came to Tortilla, the Mexican was sitting at the base of a tree, his head on his chest. Beside him was Sin Braden, hunkered with her rifle.

Buck said quietly, "Buck McKee comin' in."

"He's asleep," said Sin.

Buck groaned, "What a man!" and hooked a boot under Tortilla's cramped legs.

"They've come an' gone," said Buck. "They've burned the place down."

Tortilla Joe was suddenly wide awake. He stared at the dark buildings. "You are a beeg liar," he stated firmly.

Buck looked at Sin Braden and smiled. "What time is it, Joe?" The Mexican handed him his watch.

"They oughta be comin', soon."

Tortilla Joe jumped excitedly to his feet. He jabbed a dirty forefinger at a point across the Basin. "Look, Senor Buck. Fire, I theenk, maybe, no."

Buck stared. Far across the night and the distance, flames were springing into wild life, beating their scarlet fingers upwards through the darkness. Sin Braden's mouth was open, her breathing heavy. Jens Jones came running through the brush hollering, "McKee, Sin, where are you?"

"Here, Jens," yelled Buck.

The big dirt-man came crashing through the buckbrush. "They've double-crossed us, somewhere! They have burned that outerfit—looks to me like Bill Dighton's farmhouse an' out-buildin's! That is Bill's, ain't it, Sin?"

Sin Braden was silent for a long moment. "Sure looks like Bill's outerfit to me, Jens." She studied the three silent men. "Now what do you suppose happened? You don't reckon Jib Hobson got mixed up——?"

Jens Jones began. "Maybe he's feedin' us——"

Sin Braden interrupted savagely. "Don't say that, Jens, or I'll slap your ugly mug! Jib aims to marry my daughter an' Jib's square as a wagonbox! No, there's been some mix-up somewhere."

Jens Jones mopped his forehead: "Sorry, Sin," he murmured. "Reckon I done spoke before I done thought. No siree, Jib ain't feedin' us no lies, Sin. He's square as can be—What'd you figure happened?"

Sin looked at Buck. "What do you say, cowboy?"

Buck chewed thoughtfully on an unlighted cigarette.

Tortilla Joe spoke from around a *tortilla* he was chewing. "Frank LaWall he has changed hees mind, huh, an' he no ride here—he burn down closer shack. Thees Beel Dighton he was at the dirt camp, no? He deed not burn in fire?"

"He was at camp," said Jens Jones. "He was hittin' the sougans when we rode out. No, he ain't in that fire."

"An' him sendin' east for his bride," growled Sin Braden. "The woman should be here in a week or two. Bill took great pride in his home, I tell you; he fixed that up darn fine, jus' for the little wife. An' now when she comes there'll be only ashes——" She choked off angrily.

"Good lock he wasn't een the fire," said Tortilla Joe.

Buck was moving toward their broncs. "We better head over that way, people. There might be a chance to cut them off before they get back in the hills, but I doubt that."

"An outside chance only!" clipped Sin Braden.

They got their horses and headed north, drifting across the floor of Mad River Basin. With Sin Braden in the lead, they cut off at an angle, aiming to drive between the N Bar S and the burning buildings, hoping to catch the marauders on their trip home. Sin Braden knew the way and she hit a hard pace, her quirt rising and falling and her curses floating back at Buck and Tortilla Joe, who pounded along at her flank.

"She ees bad swearer," hollered Tortilla Joe. "She cannot go to heaven, huh, Buck? She ees swear too much."

"Don't want to go there if you head there, Tortilla," rapped out Sin Braden, grinning widely. "An' besides, who wants to float aroun' in a nightgown all the time? An' play a harp—me, I can't play nothin', I tell you. They'd gain no music by gettin' me there. Reckon I'll go down below with Buck, huh, Buck?"

"We'll start a beer joint down there," said Buck. "An' with each beer, we'll give away a free *tortilla*."

Tortilla Joe looked at him sharply. "A free *tortilla*, huh? Eef you do that, I go een as partners weeth you. . . ."

Practical Jens Jones growled. "Come back to the earth; we got a chore ahead of us——"

They used spurs and quirts liberally, but Buck knew they would never intercept the marauders. For one thing, they had been too far away from Bill Dighton's outfit;

another, LaWall and Jacobson were smart—maybe they weren't heading back to the N Bar S right off. They would leave no open trail.

His premonitions were correct; by the time they reached the foothills, the cabin was only glowing embers. And with the darkness hanging across the Basin, tracking was impossible. Buck dismounted and laid his ear to the ground. Somewhere horses were moving, coming closer. They were coming at a jarring gallop. Buck looked up at Sin Braden.

"Horses movin', somewhere?"

Tortilla Joe called, "Here they come, *Senor* Buck!"

Sin Braden pushed the Mexican's gun hurriedly aside. "Them's my dirt-men, you fool! They've seen the fire an' come to investigate." She held up her hand and called, "Hey, men, this is Sin Braden talkin'! Over this way, hombres!"

The dirt-men slid their broncs to a stop and Hans Sexton rode close to Buck.

"Now who lit this fire?" he wondered.

Buck said, crisply, "Don't know, Sexton." He tried to fit the man into this. He was a spy, yet he had slept that night. Why hadn't he been with LaWall and Dusty Jacobson and Jib Hobson?

"How come you're ridin' out at this hour?" queried Sexton.

Sin Braden spoke. "The four of us was in Oxbow, Hans. We was headin' back to camp when we see'd this fire a-blazin', so we headed this way."

"Oh, I see."

They rode to the fire. Only embers glowed where once had stood a man's future and a man's work. Buck and Sin Braden rode beside young Bill Dighton. About twenty-two, he was a dark-haired, slender youth. From the way the young fellow bounced on his work-horse, Buck saw that plainly he was an Easterner who had come to Mad River to make his home.

"Frank LaWall's done this," said Bill Dighton angrily. "He's burned my outerfit down! Well, he ain' chasin' me outa the country, I kin tell you that! I oughta get a gun an' ride over to the N Bar S——"

"An' get shot to holes," finished Buck. "Nope, Bill Dighton, just forgit that talk. Accordin' to what I've heard, you got a new young wife back east, a-headin' this way. When she gets off the Oxbow stage, I don't want the chore of tellin' her that her husban' is dead."

Bill Dighton sobered suddenly. "Guess I talked too quick, Buck. But I'm goin' rebuild, neighbor."

"That's the talk, Bill."

They split up, the homesteaders going to the cabins. They had decided that hereafter each house would be guarded every night. Sin Braden had hired a bunch of outsiders to handle fresnos and ploughs and they agreed to help the homesteaders guard their property. The job would be tedious but essential, they all agreed.

Dondo and Pone were riding wiry, short-legged cowponies. Dondo pulled his tough horse close to Buck as they rode back to camp.

"Dondo, him trail them," he said.

Pone spoke. "We can trail them in dark even, Buck."

Buck stretched and yawned. "Come daylight," he promised. After a while, Dondo came to Buck's bed, where the cowpuncher was smoking his last cigarette of the day.

"Ogo, her watch Hans Sexton. Her think Sexton fall asleep by accident. Him wake up, saddle horse—then somebody see fire. Sexton no ride to N Bar S then. Him ride with dirt-men."

Buck nodded.

"Sexton come back to camp with us. Ogo watch him from now on, huh?"

"Okay."

CHAPTER 10

NEXT MORNING, Buck and Tortilla Joe ate breakfast, seated cross-legged under a wagon. Tortilla Joe sipped noisily of his coffee and smacked his thick lips.

"We get little sleep on theese job, Buck," he declared. "My blankets, they ees theenk I am a stranger to them, huh?"

"You get too much shuteye," growled Buck.

Tortilla Joe shivered. "Down in California Baja, when I work down there on Margerita's papa's uncle's ranch, I am warm and there is time for the *siesta,* always. Here there ees only time for to eat and that ees bad."

Buck had to grin. "Gulp your Arbuckle an' put on your gun. You an' me are ridin' out to look for tracks *amigo.*"

"Seen Braden, she weel want to come, too?"

Buck shook his head. "Not if I can help it. Me, I've spent years dodgin' skirts, an' I don't want her trailin' along everywhere we go, jus' holdin' things up."

"She does not wear skirts." Tortilla Joe got to his feet. "She ees wear the pants. I go get my gun."

Buck cleaned his plate and cup. The camp was beginning to stir. Soon the night-hawk would bring in the work-horses. Sin Braden was still asleep but, as Buck watched, the big woman stirred in her blankets and sat up. She was wearing a blue nightgown. She rubbed her eyes open.

"Daylight in the swamps, you sodmovers! Rattle up to mess line an' get your dole of chuck! Come on in, you night-hawk man! A new day an' a dam to be built!"

Buck waited no longer. Unnoticed by Sin, he went into the brush where he and Tortilla had tied their horses. They stepped up and rode down the coulee, heading for the broad flat of the Basin.

They came to the mouth of the coulee and Pone and Dondo, riding their wiry ponies, came out of the buckbrush, smiling widely. "We ride out with you an' find tracks," said Dondo.

"We kill LaWall an' Jacobson some time, maybe," said Pone slowly. "Maybe no; maybe yes."

"Ogo watch Sexton," said Dondo.

They did not ride fast. They put their horses at a running-walk, riding toward Bill Dighton's farm. The sun was rising slowly and already Buck felt some of the chill leave the air. But still, the high Arizona mountains were cold. At noon, the heat would be unbearable—Buck wished they had some of it now, it was pretty chilly.

By the time they reached the farm, the sun had more warmth. Buck rolled a cigarette and looked down at the wreckage. His smoke drawing, he stepped down and stirred the ashes with one boot, his face solemn.

They left their horses rein-tied and went into the brush.

Tortilla Joe found where the marauders had tied their horses. He called to Buck and the Apaches, and they stood and studied the hoof marks. The horses, Buck noticed, had been barefoot—unshod. And an unshod horse is hard to trail. For any wild horse, crossing the trail or trotting along it, might lead a man off; the wild horse is unshod, too.

But the small Apaches had their own methods. Raised in the wilderness, they had inherited the logic and lore of their ancestors and to this they had added their own personal experiences. Dondo knelt, put his nose to the ground, sniffed of the track. He did that to others.

"These horses, they keep them in barn. Hoofs smell manure. They stand in barn. Range horse have clean hoof."

Buck knelt and sniffed. So did Tortilla. Neither of them smelled anything odd. Buck told Dondo that. The squat little Indian grinned. "You have white man's nose. Him too long, get him in trouble. Injun have short nose. Him smell good an' don't put nose in trouble."

Pone said, "Look, Dondo," and pointed at a hoof mark.

Dondo studied the mark, face impassive. Buck studied it, too, but saw nothing out of the ordinary about it. But evidently Pone and Dondo did. Dondo got to his feet. He brushed the dried grass from his bony knees.

"We ride now," he said.

The trail led away toward the hills, travelling away from the N Bar S. It was easy to follow across the Basin floor. But when it reached the rocky hills—Buck knew then he and Tortilla Joe would have to rely wholly on the Apaches.

The Mexican rubbed his nose thoughtfully. "They are going away from N Bar S, Buck," he declared. "They are not goin' toward the *rancho*. . . ."

Buck said, "Probably a trick, Tortilla Joe."

Later his conjecture was proven correct. For in a few miles the trail turned, leading back into the hills. The tracking was easy for some distance. Then, they hit a lava bed, a flat plain that ran ahead for about four miles.

Buck pulled in and looked across the lava. "Up to you from now on, Apaches," he grunted.

"We find," grunted Dondo.

Buck could see no tracks; neither could Tortilla Joe.

But evidently the Apaches could. They rode slowly, eyes glued to the rock. This went on for a few miles, then they turned suddenly, heading toward the N Bar S ranch, hidden back in the hills. Finally they came to the end of the lava. And again the tracks lay before them again —plain now on the gravelly soil.

Tortilla Joe grunted appreciation of the Apaches' trailing skill. *"Por Dios,* they accompleesh heem, Buck. Look, the tracks they are headed for the N Bar S. Now we have evidence that Frank LaWall an' two others, they burn the place down, no?"

"We know they do it all the time." Pone looked slowly across distance. "But just to make sure we follow tracks."

"Who else would do it?" asked Dondo.

Finally the trail came to the road that ran to the N Bar S. They put their broncs along it, riding at a long lope. Time and distance passed, and they were within sight of the big ranch. Pone and Dondo reined in their ponies by the thin rope tied around their broncs' underjaws.

"We no ride with you in there," said Dondo. "We stay in brush aroun' house. Maybe best we not seen but be close."

Buck agreed with that plan. There would be N Bar S riders there, and he and Tortilla Joe would be outnumbered—but, with the two savages in the brush, he would have an ace in the hole.

Dondo and Pone rode into the high buckbrush and Buck and Tortilla Joe rode up to the ranch-house. Men were coming out of the mess-shack after breakfast. Some were going to the corral and the barn for their horses. Dusty Jacobson and Jib Hobson saw them as they came out of the cook-shack.

Jacobson stopped, said, "That's McKee an' the Mex, ain't it, Jib?"

"That's them, Dusty."

"We'd better go to the house."

Buck McKee and Tortilla Joe drew their horses to a halt, there in front of the long porch. Smoke was coming upward from the stone chimney, Buck saw. That meant somebody was up and cooking breakfast.

Buck called, "Hello, the house!" and waited.

Frank LaWall came out. He squinted at them and Buck saw surprise run across his eyes.

"Kinda early to be in the saddle, ain't it, McKee?"

Buck spoke slowly. "We're trailin' some firebugs, La-Wall. They darted down last night an' burned up Bill Dighton's spread. Burned it to the ground. We struck the trail early and it led to the N Bar S."

LaWall's hawkish face was stone. "You're jumpin' at conclusions, McKee," he finally said. "Just because me an' my men are crossin' horns with the sodbusters ain't no sign I'd burn down one of them. You know, Bill Dighton was a kinda careless kid, I figure. Stopped to talk to him one evenin' an' he'd had a fire in his forge. The evenin' breeze was stirrin' it an' I could see the hot coals. That wind came up stronger in the night an' it would have lifted them coals an' blowed them into his barn. . . ."

"Hogwash!" snorted Tortilla Joe.

Dusty Jacobson and Jib Hobson had reached the house. Jacobson said, "What do these two fellows want, Frank?" and LaWall told him about Buck's accusation.

"Saw a fire down that way last night," said Jacobson. "Got up at midnight to see to that sick hoss of mine an' there was a fire over thataway, though I never gave it much thought." He looked up at Buck. "You got a nerve a-ridin' in here, McKee, an' makin' them statements!" His voice was low and husky.

Buck rasped his words angrily. "If we had enough evidence to hold in court, we'd get a warrant from Nappy Hale for you two hombres! And if Nappy wouldn't serve it, we would! We came into Mad River to stop this trouble—and by hades, we'll stop it. Have you got anythin' to say to that, Jacobson?"

Jacobson growled, "I sure have," and came forward. "Git off'n that bronc, McKee, an' back those words with your fists or get to hell off'n N Bar S sod! If I had my gun on me I'd——"

Buck's boot ground Jacobson's words short. The Justin slapped against the *segundo's* chest and drove him back. Jacobson caught himself, gasping. Buck said to Tortilla Joe, "Get your gun out an' see nobody double-deals me!"

"My gon, she ees out, *Senor* Buck."

Riders were coming on the run. Buck estimated there were about ten, twelve riders on the N Bar S. Tortilla Joe had pulled his bronc to one side, his gun covering the men. Dondo and Pone came out of the brush suddenly, rifles up. Buck saw Frank LaWall grunt when the two Apaches came out.

"You N Bar S men," growled Tortilla Joe. "Remember, keep hands from the gons, or I shoot to keel! Thees ees a feest fight, *senores,* and may the better *hombre* weens. Be good, *muchachos,* an' you leeve to see the fight." He grinned fiercely and a man backed away from him slightly. Then the man saw the rifles of Dondo and Pone, and he stared with his mouth open.

"We won't stop them," a man growled. "Me, I'd like to see that big-mouthed Jacobson get dehorned, an' *pronto.* His mouth is too big for me."

Jacobson balanced himself. He had caught his wind again, and rage flooded him. He said, "All right, McKee, fight!" and he rushed in, anger driving him. He flung a right that, if it had connected, would have pounded Buck's head from shoulders. But Buck sidestepped and planted a tough uppercut against Jacobson's jaw.

The blow staggered the *segundo.* Buck followed up relentlessly. A right fist ripped Jacobson around, almost dropped him. Buck missed with his left and Jacobson kicked him in the groin.

The pain almost doubled the tall cowpuncher. Face tight, Jacobson came ahead, fists working. Buck rode one blow, taking it on his shoulder. The second hit him and the third drove him back against the porch. Dimly he heard the cries of the N Bar S men, cheering their foreman to victory. And dimly, too, came Tortilla Joe's warning, "Back op, Buck, queek! Back op, *pronto!"*

His strength was coming back; the pain was leaving his belly. And in its stead came pouring a hot, relentless anger. He held it back, because he knew it would not help him; it would help Jacobson. He came ahead, met Jacobson, and they stood there fighting, two big men—they were two prehistoric giants, slugging there in the dim Arizona day, the dust curling around their boots.

Buck's head was unsteady. He could not stand this driving pace much longer. He felt the strength leave Jacobson's mauling fists. The big *segundo* was tiring.

"Get him, Dusty!" encouraged LaWall.

Now Buck was driving him backwards. He summoned

all his strength. His right clipped Jacobson's jaw, pivoting his head on his stout neck. A left came roaring in, almost tearing Jacobson's head from his shoulders. He went down in a flower bed, crushing the sweetpeas and wild poppies.

Breathing heavily, Buck wiped his hand across his bloody mouth. He gasped cool air into his aching lungs.

"Be good, you sons!" growled Tortilla Joe.

Suddenly, they all whirled as hoofs pounded into the sunbaked yard. Ancient Nappy Hale pulled his big stud to a sliding halt, a ten-gauge double-barrel shotgun in one hand. Buck saw he had cloth tied across the ends of the barrels. Nappy Hale's goatee bristled on his jutting jaw.

"Saw the fight from the ridge!" he blatted. "There's been enough trouble here—they ain't goin' be no more! Got ol' Betsy loaded with stove bolts an' nuts, got both dab-nabbed barrels full of hell an' destruction! First man that reaches for his cutter gets a load of the ol' lady's cookstove in his belly!"

The ancient deputy shook the gun and Buck heard the stove bolts rattle in the barrels. The cloths tied across the end kept the deadly loads in. Old Nappy looked more than ever like a goat—an old billy that had licked a label off a tin can to find he'd swallowed a dose of red pepper with it. But one thing was certain: that scattergun meant business.

And the N Bar S men knew just that. One blast from the sawed-off weapon, and stove bolts and nuts would break loose. Frank LaWall squinted up at the irate lawman. "You fire them hammers, Nappy, an' they might break the barrel off'n that gun an' scatter some hell back into you!"

This assumption was logical. Nappy Hale chewed belligerently. "But it'd hit you afore it'd hit me," he allowed steadily. "All right, Boys, the picnic is over with! McKee an' Jacobson, climb on your hosses an' head for jail!"

Frank LaWall snorted. "Jail, hades! What's wrong with you, Nappy—cain't two hombres enjoy a peaceful fight without you juggin' them?"

Nappy Hale levelled his scattergun on the big cowman. Buck heard him pull back one hammer. "One more word out of you, an' I'll run this junk-yard through your brisket!"

"Be careful," pleaded LaWall.

Jacobson spoke heavily. "You mean to say this ol' goat is goin' jug me, Frank? Goin' take me to town an' throw me in his rotten calaboose?"

Frank LaWall grinned crookedly. "He's got the scattergun, Dusty, not me. . . ." He added, "Go peaceful with him . . . I'll bail you out pronto."

"Humor the ol' billy, huh?"

One of the N Bar S punchers came up with two saddled horses. Nappy Hale had Tortilla Joe take the guns from LaWall and Jacobson, throwing them on the porch. He also took Buck's pistol, poking it in his belt.

"All right, McKee, climb on your cayuse. Hit the dust toward town, you an' Jacobson! The rest of you boys—the ones that stay behin'—just keep what little brains you have got, an' keep them pistols of yours in leather. Let's ride, hombres!"

They headed for Oxbow. Tortilla Joe reined close to Buck and said, "I go get Seen, Buck. Keep the cheen up, no?"

"Ride," said Buck.

CHAPTER 11

FRANK LAWALL rode with Jacobson. Buck took the lead, his horse pulling at the bit. Dondo and Pone headed back to the dirt camp with Tortilla Joe.

A cynical smile tugged at Buck's battered lips. He pulled in, let the two N Bar S men pass him, then held his horse a pace ahead of Nappy's. "How come you blunder in on our fight, Nappy?"

Nappy Hale snorted. He tugged his longhorn moustaches. "Blundered, hades, Buck! Peta Gomez saw the fire of Dighton's outerfit last night; she got up with one of her kids, I reckon. She done tol' me an' come daylight I pulls out, savvy? Trailed you gents to the N Bar S and come just in the right time, I'd say."

Buck was silent, momentarily. "Hard tellin' what

would've happened if you hadn't come on the scene. What do you aim to do with me an' Dusty Jacobson?"

"Try you for disturbin' the peace, by gravy!"

They came into Oxbow when the sun was pretty high. They dismounted in front of the deputy-sheriff's office, with Nappy Hale holding his scattergun on them. "March inside, you two law-breakers," he commanded.

Buck had little fear of the future. Sin Braden would bail him out. But when he saw the single cell, placed at the back of the office, the tall cowpuncher had to smile to himself.

"We both go into that cell, huh?"

"You're dab-nabbed right," declared Nappy.

"That's dangerous," joked Buck. "We might get into a fight in there an' wreck your whole jail and office, Nappy."

Nappy did not answer. They went inside. The interior was gloomy but Buck made out two bunks, one on each side of the cell. About three feet separated them. Dusty Jacobson cursed and sat down, glaring at Nappy Hale, who swung shut the log door with the small porthole in it.

"Your hearin' is set for this afternoon." Nappy Hale studied his dollar watch. "Aroun' two, I reckon. I gotta eat an' rest up some yet."

"Don't hurry," said Buck lazily.

Nappy stumped outside, slamming the outer door behind him. Dusty Jacobson lay down and turned his back to Buck, who sat on his bunk and regarded the cowman laconically. An hour passed and Dusty Jacobson slept, his snores echoing through the cell. Buck grimaced and lay down and dozed.

Noon brought two things: A tray of dinner and Tortilla Joe. The heavy Mexican grinned widely. "You are in good place, Buck, but the company—ah, that ees bad. Seen is comin' in pronto; me an' Dondo ride ahead of her, to tell you."

"Dondo?"

Dondo's voice came through the hole. "Me too small look in, Buck."

Nappy Hale said, "All right, Tortilla Joe; you an' the Injun make tracks now. My prisoners gotta eat their chow."

Twenty minutes later, Sin Braden breezed in, accompanied by Janice. When she saw Buck she laughed and slapped her thick thigh. "We'll get you outa here plumb pronto, Buck," she growled. "Come a short time, an' we'll have your hearin'. I'll go good any sum the judge sets up."

"Who's the judge?"

"Why, Nappy, of course. He's town constable, deputy sheriff, justice of the peace, jailer, county tax collector—"

Buck interrupted. "An' that ol' billy-goat tol' me an' Tortilla Joe he was just a county pensioner! An' he said he didn't do any law work, he just packed the badge because he got a bigger pension as a deputy!"

Sin smiled widely. Janice's eyes twinkled. "He tells that to all the boys," said Janice. "He looks harmless . . . but he isn't."

Sin looked at Dusty Jacobson, who sat on his cot eating his dinner. "You sure busted up that homely son's homely mug. An' he didn't miss no hits he sent toward you, either, it looks like."

"Next time," said Jacobson, "we'll settle this with guns, McKee."

Buck did not answer. Jacobson's low voice was laden with hatred. He was one who could not joke, would let a hate lie in him and poison him. Buck mentally marked him as a dangerous man thereafter; if it came to a gun-tussle, he would shoot to kill . . . much as he disliked that thought.

"That's up to you," said Buck.

The sincerity of Dusty Jacobson's answer had also driven the smiles from Sin and Janice. The elderly woman's face dropped into hard, thoughtful lines. Janice's pretty young lips were pursed in disdain.

Finally Sin said, "See you at the trial, Buck," and they left.

Nappy Hale had appointed Franco Gomez as bailiff. The trial was held under the big cottonwood tree across the street. Old Nappy sat on a high bench, a table in front of him. He used a gnarled cottonwood bole as a gavel. He beat the table so hard it almost capsized.

"Bring in the prisoners, Franco," he ordered.

Franco Gomez scurried toward the jail. Peta Gomez put her head on Tortilla Joe's shoulder and started to weep. The fat Mexican stroked her greasy hair and caught the spicy odor of garlic and red peppers about her person.

He had an idea that Peta liked this. It was anything but delightful to Tortilla Joe.

"Here comes Franco weeth Buck an' Jacobson. Franco, he maybe get mad, no, if he sees you have your head there, huh?"

"You would like that, no? Then I go weeth you, huh? Me an' my *muchachos*."

Tortilla Joe considered that carefully. He would have to evade the trap some way. Finally he found his way out. "I am seengle mans," he said slowly. "I am goin' stay seengle, too. No woman, she ees good enough for Tortilla Joe."

Peta jerked her head up indignantly and he lost the scent of peppers and garlic. "Peta ees not good enough for you, no?"

"The preesoners, they are comin'," said the Mexican, anxious to change the subject.

Peta Gomez cursed under her breath at Tortilla Joe and all men in general. Tortilla Joe moved completely out of the range of the garlic by taking a seat beside Sin Braden, who sat with Jens Jones and Janice. He said, as Buck went by, "Keep the cheen up, *amigo*," and he patted his holstered .45.

"No gun-play, Tortilla!" snapped Sin Braden. "That would just make it worse an' somebody'd get killed."

Tortilla Joe crossed his legs, resigning himself to fate. "But why did Nappy Hale peench them?"

"Nappy just wants to show the N Bar S he's still boss of Mad River Basin," informed Sin Braden. "He only did it to show Frank LaWall his pants fit too tight. Nappy an' me got the whole thing cooked up—both Buck an' Dusty Jacobson get out under peace bond, an' that's it."

The scatteration of witnesses and spectators came to attention as the gnarled gavel beat the table. "Hear ye, hear ye," intoned Nappy Hale. He added something else about "the great territory of Arizona, sixteenth judicial district," and then he called the prisoners to the bar.

"How do you plead?" he demanded of Jacobson. "You're charged with bustin' the peace up, an' you can plead guilty or not guilty. Which be she?"

"Not guilty."

Nappy snapped, "You forgot somethin', feller!"

Jacobson was puzzled. "What'd you mean, Nappy?"

Nappy's gavel pounded angrily. Some person in the back of the assembly said, "He wants you to call him 'His Honor,' Dusty. Humor the ol' goat."

Nappy Hale glared at the crowd. "If'n I fin' out who said that, I'll jail him for contempt of court. All right, Jacobson, how do you plead?"

"Not guilty ... Your Honor."

"An' you, McKee?"

Buck had to smile. "Guilty, Your Honor."

Old Nappy Hale's pigeon-chest expanded. "Now that's the way a model prisoner addresses the court," he declared, glaring at Jacobson. "Buck McKee, I hereby put you under a peace bond to the extent of five hundred dollars. Should you get into court again during your stay in Mad River Basin, you forfeit such bond—that is, if somebody puts it up for you. An' if it ain't posted, you go to jug for ten days, beginnin' right pronto."

"I'll post his bond," said Sin Braden.

Nappy Hale spoke to Franco Gomez. "The lady over there says she'll post the prisoner's bail, bailiff. Get her name and address right pronto an' get some security if'n she ain't got the cash on her."

"I'll pay cash," declared Sin Braden. "But I want a receipt for it."

"Me, I cannot write," said Franco Gomez, shrugging.

Spectators laughed. Judge Nappy Hale pounded again. Order was finally restored. "I'll write the receipt." Franco Gomez brought him the bills which Nappy Hale counted slowly, wetting his thumb each time. "The sum is correct, madam. The prisoner is in your custody." He settled his pale eyes on Dusty Jacobson. "So you want a jury trial, huh? That means you go back to jail until I set a date for your trial an' after I select a jury."

"How long will that be?" asked Jacobson, his voice not too steady.

"Might be tomorrow ... might be next week. Sometimes the wheels of justice work awful slow. Of course, I could set bail an' you could be free until your trial comes up. How would that be?"

"How much bail?" asked Frank LaWall.

Nappy Hale turned his eyes on the N Bar S owner. "Are you the prisoner's lawyer?"

"No."

"Then keep your mug closed, or I'll fine you for contempt of court. The bail, Jacobson, would be ten thousand dollars, cash, posted immediately."

Frank LaWall could stand it no longer. "Nappy, you damned ol'——"

"Twenty dollars fine for LaWall," clipped Nappy. "Disturbin' the court. Collect it, Franco." The old man dragged his scattergun out from behind his chair and Buck heard the stove bolts rattle. Franco Gomez, his face pale, sidled up to Frank LaWall, keeping to one side so his fat body would not shield the cowman.

"You hear what Hizzoner say?" said Franco, his voice unsteady. "Me, I do not like to do this, Frank, but he make me!"

"Here's your cash," growled Frank LaWall. "Dusty, for your sake, change your plea, you damned cow-pusher."

"I plead guilty," declared Jacobson hurriedly.

Nappy Hale's leathery face broke into a smile. "Now, that's better, cowboy." He placed the N Bar S *segundo* also under a five hundred dollar peace bond, which Frank LaWall paid. Hale rapped with the cottonwood bole again. "Court is dismissed until a future date. Will the participants get to hell out of town an' stay out as long as possible—or come in only when they need some groceries or for their mail?"

"Don't forget," said Franco Gomez, "they can come een to buy the wheeskey an' wine, at my place—we agreed on that before the trial, no?"

"Yeah, I remember."

Frank LaWall came by and said, "Make danged sure you send that bail money into the county seat, Nappy."

Nappy glared at him.

LaWall and Jacobson and their punchers got their horses and rode out.

Buck and Sin and Tortilla Joe went into Franco Gomez' saloon, while Janice stayed in the post office. According to the postmaster, the stage should have been in by now, and the mail was on it. So they had decided to stay and get the mail.

"We have good trial, no?" asked Franco, wiping off two clean whiskey glasses. He slid them across the counter with a bottle of Old Crow. Then he handed Tortilla Joe a glass and a bottle of *tequila*. Buck poured a jigger of whiskey but Sin Braden drank hers right out of the bottle.

"Good for who?" asked Sin, belligerently.

Franco read the trouble-sign in her eyes and remained silent. Tortilla Joe raised his *tequila* glass and squinted over the rim. "Here she ees come the stage, Buck."

"Uh-huh."

Through the greasy, fly-specked window they could see the Concord come in. The four sorrel horses, strung out two-abreast, came rolling down the hill, dust rising lazily under their hoofs and from the wheels. The driver braked them to a halt in front of the post office and threw down the mail sack to the man.

"There's some packages in the back.

"No passenger, huh?" grunted Franco Gomez.

Sin Braden downed another slug from the bottle. "The postmaster's takin' some suitcases outa the boot," she mumbled. "There must be a passenger on there but if there is he's sure takin' his sweet time about gettin' out, huh?"

"Maybe somebody they ees ships in their suitcases?" said Tortilla Joe.

Buck watched with a casual indifference. Finally, he saw a crutch push its way out of the stage, saw another come out. Their owner, still hidden, placed them both solidly, then swung out on the ground. Buck lowered his glass and stared.

"Are my eyes seein' right?" he asked Tortilla Joe.

The Mexican squinted. "I guess so, *Senor* Buck. It looks like him to me, too, but the deestance, she ees long. . . ."

Sin Braden slammed her bottle so hard on the bar that she put a dent in the hardwood. Franco Gomez hurriedly inspected the damage. "You have to pay for that," he said sternly. "That bar, she ees come aroun' the Horn, an'——"

But Sin wasn't listening. "Whoopee," she cried, "look what crawled out of that doghouse on wheels! Ol' Colonel Henry S. Braden, hisself! Why, the ol' jackass——" She cupped her hands to her big mouth. "Hey, Colonel, this way!"

Colonel Henry S. Braden stared at the saloon. "You in there, Sin?"

"This way, Colonel."

Obese face beaming, the army man crutched toward the saloon, came through the swinging doors. And then Sin Braden had him in her arms, crutches and all. The thing was quite a mix-up after that. Colonel Henry S. Braden lost one crutch and bumped his bum leg against the floor. He hollered and cursed and Tortilla Joe got his crutch under him again. The colonel adjusted himself properly and looked at Buck and Tortilla Joe. "So you finally got here, huh?"

"Us, een the flesh," said Tortilla Joe.

Colonel Henry S. Braden glared at the drinks on the bar. His long nose wrinkled in apparent disdain. His glacial eyes clashed with those of Franco Gomez. Then he broke loose.

"Get out of this bar, you three! Whiskey and *tequila,* the ruin of man and woman alike! Get out, I tell you, and we'll talk where the air is free from this vile smell, this terrible odor!"

"They owe me some money," cried Franco Gomez.

The colonel showered the bar with silver. "That should reimburse you, pig." He shooed them outside, balancing himself precariously on his crutches. But, as they went, unnoticed by the irate army man, Sin Braden managed to stuff a whiskey bottle under her shirt.

"For snake-bite," she told Buck.

Once outside, the colonel breathed deeply. "Lord, such good air, and you leave it by entering such a vile den of sin. Now what have you got to say for yourself, Tortilla Joe?"

Tortilla Joe shrugged. "Noddin'," he said.

CHAPTER 12

FRANK LAWALL rode out of Oxbow that day with the fine white heat of anger inside. One pit of this anger was stoked by the thought that he had always underestimated old Nappy Hale. Never before had the oldster gone to such violent ends to uphold the law. Heretofore he had always regarded Nappy Hale as a somewhat harmless, though bullheaded, old man.

He looked at Jacobson and said, "I had that ol' billy goat pegged wrong."

Jacobson ran a broad hand over his swollen cheek. "Hard to tell about a man," he said. "Me, I'd much rather have the job of judgin' a horse...."

"Now why didn't Sexton ride with us last night?" demanded Frank LaWall. "You don't figure that son aims to rabbit out fast on us, do you, Dusty?"

"I don't know," said Jacobson.

Frank LaWall ran this thought across his mind. Mentally he rolled it and examined it for flaws and found none. Hans Sexton was in too deep; if he told now, the dirtmen would string him up. "Maybe they were thick in camp," he said, "an' Sexton was afraid to pull out to come to us, figurin' maybe some of them might see him an' wonder an' decide to trail him."

"He's playin' a tough game," said Dusty Jacobson. "If'n that dirt-man fin' out about him——" He drew his forefinger suggestively across his throat.

Frank LaWall abandoned the thought of Sexton, and ran his mind into the work ahead. Coldly he pushed the thoughts through him, discarding those he did not like or want, holding those he thought appropriate.

Would Bill Dighton leave the Basin now that his property had been destroyed? Would the cold fear of marauding night-riders scare other hoemen from Mad River? LaWall wondered on this and decided the next few days would tell the tale. By that time those farmers who were leaving would have packed their belongings into wagons and made tracks out of the level land. This was a warm spot in the big cowman.

And if this hegira were too slow, if enough farmers did not move, then he would hit at the dams, blowing them up. Here would be the tough phase of the struggle. So far no blood had been shed on Mad River, save that caused by hard knuckles. This had not settled down to gun-play yet. But he knew that if he and his riders hit a dam, that dam would be guarded—and guns would undoubtedly talk . . . and men might die.

He told his plan to Dusty Jacobson, who said—"Here is my lay, Frank. Buck McKee an' me cain't live together on this earth . . . they ain't enough space for the two of us." The pride of this big man with the broken face was a strong, vital force, and Frank LaWall felt the imprint of its power. "That's my personal side of it. The other side is one with money: You pay me top wages so I ride for you."

"I asked your opinion," growled Frank LaWall, "not your life history...."

Dusty Jacobson held back his temper. He was silent for some time. "They'll have guards posted and there'll be a tussle. Somebody's apt to get killed. But the thing levels down to this: You want this range and you're out to get it and there will have to be bloodshed if you are going to get it. Personally, I don't think you'll win, Frank."

"You're blunt," said LaWall grudgingly.

"You can't hold back the push of Time. Sooner or later this land is goin' to be settled into farms."

"An' when it does, I'll be ownin' those farms. I'll raise feed down there an' run my cattle back on the bench land and the foothills. Don't get this wrong, Dusty. Sin Braden had somethin' when she started this irrigation. With her out of the way, and with the basin land mine, I'd still carry on that water scheme. With the settlers gone, I could, in a matter of time, get all the bottom land filed on, and get it in my name. That's the lay from here."

"You might win . . . with that idea," admitted Jacobson. "You can bet I'm with you all the way, Frank. Buck McKee'll pay to me sooner or later."

"Let's hope it's *sooner*."

They slanted around a bend and then Frank LaWall was suddenly reining in, his sliding bronc kicking up gravel. The N Bar S owner had his rifle out, bringing it to his shoulder. Far on the heights, a rider was moving toward the rocks. He was a small man, hanging to his horse's mane, and he was about half a mile away.

"Trailin' us," growled LaWall. "One of those damned Apaches. I'll——"

Dusty Jacobson grabbed his boss' rifle and pulled it down. "No, Frank, no!" he said huskily. "Don't kill that Apache! Don't ever lift a gun against an Apache, 'cept in self defense!"

Frank LaWall cursed, his eyes on the spot where Dondo had disappeared in the rocks. "I'd a-got him if'n you hadn't wrecked my aim," he said angrily. "Them danged redskins been trailin' me too much lately. I've seen 'em a number of times, Dusty. Some one of these days——"

Jacobson spoke slowly. "I'll tell you what would happen, Frank. I've seen it before, a number of times. You'd kill one of those Apaches. Either Dondo or Pone. The other would see it, no doubt; they always work in pairs. Nobody'd say anythin'. You'd think the matter had blown over. Then some mornin' we'd find you stiff in your blankets, your throat cut from ear to ear. Cut so fast and so expertly you'd never even know how you come to die...."

Frank LaWall stuck his rifle back into scabbard. "I'd have somethin' to say about that," he said strongly. "No redskin is gettin' the best of Frank LaWall. I've killed them before, an' I'll prob'ly kill more of them."

"These Apaches," said Dusty Jacobson, "are different Indians, Frank." He saw there was no use in taking the argument further so he fell back into silence and settled deep in his saddle.

They came to a drift-fence, and LaWall drew them to a halt. He gave his orders and his riders turned and rode to their jobs. LaWall and Dusty Jacobson rode to the N Bar S. When they came in sight of the ranch, a fierce pride of ownership gripped Frank LaWall. The *mozo* was at the toolshed.

Dusty Jacobson went to the barn with the old *mozo* and helped him unsaddle the two horses. "Saw one of them Injuns today," said the oldster. "Back in the bresh, Dusty. One of the women—this Ogo girl, I reckon they call her."

Jacobson nodded. Out of the open door he could see Frank LaWall at the porch. War Chief came running to meet his father, who picked him up and put him on his shoulder. The child was dressed in the regalia of his mother's tribe: he had on buckskin trousers, a buckskin jacket and his hair was braided with a bright feather in the black coil.

LaWall carried him into the house and set him down.

"Me, I chase buffalo," declared War Chief.

Feather Eagle came from the kitchen. Frank LaWall caught the odor of spices and the healthy aroma of something boiling. The squaw had been trained to the white man's way of cooking in a Jesuit school when she was a child. She had adopted other habits and traits of the white man there, too.

"What happened down in Oxbow?" she asked.

"They put Dusty an' Buck McKee on peace bond. Five hundred dollars. Ol' Nappy acted as judge."

"You went Dusty's bond?"

"Sure, who else would?"

"What if he jumps it—leaves the country?"

Frank LaWall laughed huskily. "Dusty won't jump it, woman. He's in this deep, and he knows his cut if we win. And besides, there's McKee. . . . And what t'hell is five hundred bucks when you got a quarter million at stake? When you gamble, gamble big or don't splurge."

She shook her heavy head and the ornaments in her dark hair made a small sound. "God can see, and man cannot." She had control of herself now and again he felt her shut him from her. "God can see, and we hope He is good to us." She went back to her kitchen.

War Chief said, "I'm going out to play, daddy."

Frank LaWall said. "All right, son," and the boy went out, slamming the door behind him. His father turned and went out the back door. He climbed the hill slowly, his wife's words in him, and finally he reached the top. There he stood in among the huge sandstone rocks and looked at Mad River Basin below him.

The land pitched, rose, fell. Standing there, he could see the puff of dust, there where the fresnos and ploughs were tearing the sod, miles away. And there was Mad River, too; far away and boiling, stirring. The river, he thought, was like his memories, his thoughts.

CHAPTER 13

DONDO HAD already left Oxbow, according to Peta Gomez. "I see heem ride toward the dirt camp," said the fat Mexican woman. Sin Braden and Buck went to the back of the saloon where Franco Gomez had an extra saddle horse and saddle. They saddled the beast—an old iron-grey gelding—and helped the colonel up. The old horse slouched, one hip down, and contemplated the ground.

Colonel Henry S. Braden swore under his breath. "Come into town expecting you to be at work and here I find you all in the saloon. How do you account for that, McKee? Here I pay you top wages, too."

"So far, we have not got no money," said Tortilla Joe.

"The end of the month ain't come yet," roared the colonel. "Here, tie my crutches behind my saddle, Tortilla Joe." He shifted in his saddle, rocking his heavy bulk back and forth. "Adjust the stirrup to my good leg—no, don't touch my other leg, damn you! Yeah, I came here against my doctor's order! Danged ol' skate, must be about two hundred years old. Can't a man get a suitable mount in this so-called town?"

Buck was scowling as he hit leather. For one thing, he didn't like Dondo riding off alone—sooner or later, he figured, the little Apache would stop a bullet. He had a deep consideration for the little redskin and his bravery. And the second item that bothered him was Colonel Henry S. Braden.

With the colonel on the scene, anything would be apt to happen. . . . The fiery army man had only one plan in his system, only one approach to a problem: that was to tie into the opposition and beat him down. Well, that was all right in the army, where the colonel had trained fighters, but the sodbusters were not fighting men—they were just poor, everyday people trying to find a place where they could make a suitable living for themselves and their families.

"Tell me about this trial, Sin?" demanded the colonel.

Sin Braden told him the whole story, helped now and then by Janice. And when the story had been told, the colonel blew up. "I can say this; we ride over to the N Bar S immediately and call that rascal's hand——"

Buck had stood enough. Sooner or later, there would have to be a showdown with the army officer—and it might just as well be now, he figured. "Close your big mouth, Colonel. You hired me an' Tortilla Joe to run this outerfit. We either run it, or else we get off the job."

"Si," said Tortilla Joe. "Ees that clear, Colonel?"

Colonel Henry S. Braden stared with bulging eyes. "This," he said weakly, "is mutiny!"

"We are not een the army now," corrected Tortilla Joe. "So thees cannot be the mutiny, no? But Buck, what he say go for me, too."

The colonel considered that. Buck saw his temper die

down. "I'm a sick man," he said. "I need your help, boys. But if this was the army——" His lower lip stiffened. "If this was the army, I'd have you horsewhipped and——"

"But this ain't the army," put in Buck McKee. "This is our show, Colonel. If we rode over to the N Bar S an' forced LaWall an' Jacobson we'd be workin' right into their hands—when the smoke cleared away, we might have won the gun fight but the N Bar S would have the law on their side, an' I doubt if we could hold what we won."

"Buck hit the nail," said Sin Braden.

"We oughta get some cavalry in here," mumbled Colonel Henry S. Braden. "With them, we could wipe out these rebels, these outcasts——"

Buck sighed and winked at Sin, who closed one eye in return.

The colonel was silent the rest of the trip, nursing his temper and his bum leg. He jogged along on the old horse. The others had to hold in their mounts to keep from outdistancing him. Finally they got to the dam . . . the afternoon was far gone. They sat their horses and looked at the teams and men toiling below.

"A great work," said the colonel. "This valley needs farmers and will bloom like the proverbial rose, once water caresses its sandy surface."

Buck and Jens Jones walked out on the fill. The dam was going up nicely; Jones said this was the biggest one they had constructed to that date and perhaps would be the biggest on Mad River range. Hans Sexton was bossing the dump wagons, telling them where to drop their loads. He grinned crookedly at Buck and rubbed his split nose, the scar showing clearly.

"Far as we know, young Bill Dighton must've pulled out, McKee. He left camp at noon, an' we ain't seen him since."

Buck studied him. "What do you mean? He left his team an' wagon behin' him; I saw them in camp."

Sexton shrugged. "He ain't aroun'." He declared. "He saddled his horse an' rode away. That fire hit him hard, fellow. Me, I figure he flew the coop before this trouble got serious, an' bullets started to fly. Two other men left, too; hooked up to their wagons and went home to load up an' get out of Mad River. When Dighton's house caught afire, or whatever happened to it—why, they got col' feet, the softies, an' decided to drift."

"Who left?" asked Jens Jones.

"Tim Pinkey was one, Nye Thorp the other." The man pointed across the valley. "See their wagons way off yonderly?"

Buck could barely make out the two wagons because of the distance and the descending dusk. He and Jens Jones moved out of hearing range of Hans Sexton. They squatted and Buck drew his finger through the damp earth.

"That'll help Frank LaWall at lot," he said slowly. "He'll burn another place, likely. A couple get scared an' move out, he figures, will show that this burnin' Dighton down did some good, an' he'll be more liable to try more fire."

"We'll trap him," declared Jones.

Buck scowled deeply. "Dang it, we sure had tough luck—missin' him the last time." He doubled up his hand into a hard fist. "But Bill Dighton ain't left, Jones. You can bet on that. I'm afraid for that young fellow. He might've took it into his head to go over to the N Bar S an' brace LaWall or Dusty Jacobson."

"He's got a temper, Buck."

They went down to the dirt-camp. The teamsters were coming in now. Horses were splashing in the water-hole, burying their muzzles in the water.

Buck spoke to Sin Braden. "Bill Dighton's left, Sin."

"Where do you suppose he went?"

"I don't know."

Buck went down the coulee on foot. He said, "Ogo," and the squaw came from the wild rosebushes, carrying a rifle as long as she was tall. "You stay here on guard, huh?"

She nodded.

"You see Bill Dighton, huh?"

"Him go toward N Bar S. Pone see. Pone follow him." She looked at the sky and pointed. "Sun, him there, Buck."

Buck thought, *He left about three, I guess*. He thanked the squaw, who moved back into the brush. So Pone was following Dighton. Pone, he figured, would see that the youngster kept shy of trouble.

Buck went to his horse, saddled the tired beast. Colonel Henry S. Braden came up. He cleared his throat twice.

"Ahem, McKee, a word, please. Perhaps, this afternoon,

my blessed tongue and my cursed temper joined forces too rapidly, causing a slight misunderstanding between us. If such were the case, you have my apologies, sir."

Buck smiled thinly. "You tryin' to tell me you talked too fast an' you said too much—is that it, Colonel?"

"Well, if you put it that way, yes."

Buck stepped into saddle. "We'll get along all right, if you stay out of my way," he said. He wasn't going to give the high-handed old robber an inch.

"Where you going?"

"Out to look for some sheep," said Buck.

He left the colonel standing there. The army man was frowning; there were no sheep on this range and his limited sense of humor did not catch the drift of Buck's witticism. Buck smiled and touched his horse with his spurs.

He rode toward the N Bar S. He rode the ridges, studying the terrain below him; no horse or rider moved on it. When he came to Piney Ridge, Jib Hobson sat his bronc in the brush, hidden until he called to Buck, who rode up to him.

"What's on your mind, Jib?"

"Pone's over yonder, Buck; acrost the hill. He's got young Bill Dighton. Bill was headin' for the N Bar S, an' I spotted him. Me, I got up on the sandstones, an' Bill comes ridin' along under me—I beefed him with my shortgun. Didn't figure you wanted him to get into any trouble, McKee."

"An' then what?"

"Pone was a-trailin' Bill, so he come up. I pulled outa the picture 'cause Bill don't know I'm workin' for Janice an' her mamma. Reckon I'd hit back for camp an' then I saw you a-headin' this way."

Buck clipped his words. "You're ridin' a wild horse, Jib, an' it's a long ways to the ground. Right now some N Bar S hand might be on some ridge watchin' us through field glasses! An' you know what would happen to you if'n that happened don't you?"

"I'm no danged fool," growled Jib. He swivelled in his saddle and looked along the darkening skyline. "But it's for Janice's sake, McKee. Sooner this gets over, the sooner we can marry up an' live respectable lives. I got a gun an' I know how to use it."

"Me an' Tortilla Joe'll be aroun' close when you holler," promised Buck.

Jib Hobson grinned crookedly. "I might need you, Buck. Well, I understan' we hol' another pow-wow tomorrow night, an' Hans Sexton is suppose to be there. I'll meet you in a few days—day after tomorrow in the afternoon—down by that lone pine on Skunk Crick."

"How come they hit Bill Dighton's house instead of Dirty Henry?" asked Buck.

Jib Hobson's eyes were steady. "I'm plumb sorry about givin' you that bad horn, Buck. But sure enough, they intended to hit Dirty Henry, then, on the last minute, Frank LaWall changes his mind. I'd hoped to get free of them an' ride to warn you, but I never had a chance. You gotta believe me, Buck."

"Your word's good," murmured Buck.

Hobson rode back into the brush. Ten minutes later, Buck saw him on a high ridge, heading for the N Bar S. He was skylined for a minute and then the ridge hid him. Buck rode to where Pone was coming out of a gulley with Bill Dighton slumped in his saddle. He lifted his hand and said, "Buck McKee, comin' in, Pone."

Evidently Pone had not been sure of his identity because of the encroaching darkness. For when Buck rode up the small Apache was returning his big gun to the holster that hung against his hip.

"Hi, Buck."

Buck said, "Hi, Injun," and looked at Bill Dighton. "Now what t'hades happened to you, Bill?"

Bill Dighton's young face broke into a pained smile. "Me, I got the bit in my teeth an' I decided to hightail it over to the N Bar S an' call LaWall. Well, I was ridin' through the sandstones, and my light went out——Next thing I knew, Pone here was pourin' water outa his canteen over me." He lifted a hand and gingerly explored his swollen head. "Pone claims a rock fell on me. Loosened from the sandstones an' hit me plumb center."

Pone grinned. "Rock fall. Rock smack him. Him go dizzy, go sleep."

Buck nodded. "Could happen, I reckon."

"Seems funny to me," declared Bill Dighton. "Danged funny, McKee."

Buck made his voice serious. "Next time, Bill, you come

to either me or Tortilla, don't bat off alone, savvy? You mighta got killed. Then what would that little girl do without you?"

"It made me mad, Buck."

"That ain't gonna win for us, Bill. What'll win for us is that we all unite, we stick together. That's the only way we can win. Now Tim Pinkey an' Nye Thorp have packed up and left. You know what that means, don't you?"

"Well, I got ideas."

"I means that when Frank LaWall burned your place down, he drove out two settlers. He got results, he did. But if they had stayed, an' nobody'd left—well, then LaWall would have seen the fire didn't do any good, an' he might've quit that scheme. But, with them leavin', you can expect another fire 'most any night now."

Dighton was seriously quiet. "That's my thoughts, too, Buck." He stuck out his hand and Buck took it. "All right, partner, I won't go off on any mad-hat scheme alone. You got my word, Buck."

"Your word's good, Bill."

Bill Dighton loped ahead toward camp. Pone guided his wiry pony close to Buck. "You see Jib, huh?"

Buck nodded.

Pone smiled. "Jib slug him. Stop him."

"Best thing he could do. Only thing he could do, I reckon."

The wiry little Indian galloping beside him, the tall cowboy gave himself over to his thoughts.

Janice had smiled lazily, sleepily, and he had thought of Jib Hobson, there in the N Bar S camp. Her smile was for Jib, and for their future. She was waiting, and Jib was waiting, and Time held the strings. Time would pull the net in and bring this all together and settle it. And then the whole thing would unfold, would disintegrate, and the Basin would be free.

He took his thoughts from this. He said, "An' where is Dondo, Pone?"

"Him ride high. Him on ridge. Him see you come. Him watch at N Bar S. Someday him kill Frank LaWall."

"LaWall might have somethin' to say about that."

"Dondo kill him." Pone shook his head positively.

A rider came out of the night and said, "Thees she ees Tortilla Joe, *hombres*. Leather the gons an' I come to you."

"Come on," growled Buck. "Nobody'll shoot you, you fool!"

Frank LaWall rode the range that morning, and Jib Hobson and Dusty Jacobson rode with him. The big man was in a tight, secretive mood. But things, he reasoned, had brightened a little—some of the farmers had found it best to move out, and more might follow . . . with a little urging.

"What about this ol' gent—ol' Colonel Braden?" asked Dusty Jacobson slowly.

LaWall put his weight against the back of his saddle. He said, "That damned ol' nanny goat! Him an' that bum leg get in my way an' I'm breakin' his neck. I spent a stretch in the army years back, the cavalry. I got my guts full of their brass. Ol' Stiff Buttons rub my fur an' I'll dehorn him with the flat side of my six-shooter."

"He's got lots of influence, though," said Dusty Jacobson. "He might call in the cavalry if things break too tight."

LaWall scowled. "Nearest post is Fort James, an' that's almost two hundred miles away." He rubbed his bewhiskered jaw thoughtfully. "Hardly think that will happen. Of course, a man never knows."

Jacobson grunted, "One of them danged Ilaks up yonder on the ridge. Jus' caught sight of him as he ducked into the brush. Looked like the one they call Pone. Me, I don't like to see them heathens aroun', much less know that one is trailin' me all the time."

Frank LaWall was studying the pine trees on the ridge behind them, his eyes small behind his lids. "Me, I don't cotton to no redskin on my trail, either. There'll be a time when I sight one of them two off in some lone country, an' by hell I'll send a bullet through him an' bury him there. That-a-way ol' Nappy Hale'll never find his carcass, an' there'll be no more said."

"You forgot one thing," said Jib Hobson.

"Yeah? An' that?"

"You might notch off one of them, yes. . . . You bury him. Sure, Nappy Hale or no white man'll find the grave, but the other Ilaks will. An' when they do, they'll read your sign and some night you'll wake up with a slit throat."

LaWall grinned crookedly. "I'll chance that, Jib."

They were running N Bar S cattle out of the low

country, turning them toward the higher ridges at the base of the mountains. There were still some grassy mesas and natural pastures that the cattle had not found. Graze was growing poor on the Basin land; when the settlers had strung fences, cattle had been forced to forage on poorer pasture—the farmers fenced up the best grass.

Up yonder, the snow had melted later because of the high altitude; therefore there was still grass. But cattle, as a rule, do not care for brush and high plains—they want level land or land that is rolling, not sharp and drawn into ravines. The work was slow and tedious. The afternoon came and started to slip away into history.

Jib Hobson rode with the wild abandon of a born cowman. He was part of his horse, running through the high brush; when his pony pivoted to head off a wild cow, Jib sat a tight saddle. But he never allowed any of the N Bar S men to get above him. From up there a man could shoot another down easily.

He saw Pone once. The pygmy Apache had recognized him despite the distance; he had lifted a bronzed arm in greeting. He had been on a ridge far back in the mountains. Jib knew that nobody was getting higher than the redskin. Pone would see to that.

Frank LaWall had pulled to a halt. He waved Jib in and the youth rode down-slope. Dusty Jacobson came from a gulley. The N Bar S *segundo* sat and looked upward at some cattle.

"Got a few up high," he murmured.

Frank LaWall said, "Yeah, a few. . . ." and was silent. He was looking at the Basin, sleeping there below, and his thoughts were many. He swept his gaze to the south and saw the puff of dust left by the fresnos and ploughs and he held his eyes on that for a long moment. Then he looked at them and something was in his eyes, mirroring his thoughts. "Follow me."

But he did not lead them toward the N Bar S.

Dusty Jacobson called, "Where to, Frank?"

"A visit," said LaWall.

"Visit who?" asked Jacobson.

"Max Ayers," said LaWall.

Jacobson said, "Oh, I see."

Jib Hobson thought, *So that's the destination.* Max Ayers had settled at the base of Slope Hill where he had built out of pine-pole logs. He had Mrs. Ayers, a dark-haired Hungarian, and they had come from Toledo, Ohio. They had three children, too; young Max, about nineteen, and Margaret and Jennie, the youngest, about ten. And, at the present time, the father was at the dirt camp. He stayed there nights, too, because the ride back and forth to his farm was too long.

"We pick on the women an' kids when the ol' man is gone," said Jib Hobson.

Frank LaWall looked at him.

Twenty minutes later they rode into the yard of the Ayers farm. Margaret was milking the cow at the corral and she hollered, "Hey, Ma, get the shotgun!" Jennie, who was feeding the chickens, stared at them, then dropped her wheat-pail and spilled the feed, the chickens falling to with great clucking and ado.

"Ma," she hollered.

"They don't trust us." Jib Hobson smiled.

"Where's the boy?" asked Dusty Jacobson. "Where's young Max?"

Frank LaWall said, "He's aroun', somewhere."

"Yeah," said Jacobson. "He might be in the barn, aimin' a rifle at us—or a scattergun, maybe."

"You sound afraid," said Jib Hobson.

"He's on the porch," informed Frank LaWall. "Him an' his mother are both there."

They rode up to the porch. "What are you doin' on our land?" demanded the boy. He was a husky lad; big for his age.

Frank LaWall studied him and his mother with a lazy indifference. Dusty Jacobson sat in his saddle and looked at Margaret and Jennie, who had hurried from their chores. Margaret had a milkpail, about one-half full, and Jennie had some eggs cradled in her apron.

Neither Mrs. Ayers or young Max had any weapons.

"Dang, we're sorry, ma'am," said Frank LaWall, taking off his hat. "But we figured sure this place was empty. We done heard you folks had drifted the country the last day or so, figurin' this was no place for homesteaders to settle. We rode up here expectin' this house to be vacant."

"Oh, you did, did you?" stated Margaret.

"Margaret, be quiet." Mrs. Ayers spoke to Frank LaWall. "And what makes you think we would leave?"

"Yeah," declared young Max. "What makes you think that, Big Mouth?"

LaWall glared at the youth. "You've got a sort of big mouth yourself, son," he said. He looked at the housewife. "Well, since Bill Dighton's place burned down, a number of homesteaders left, thinkin' maybe fire was like a fever —their shacks might catch it next."

Mrs. Ayers' voice was glacial. "I can assure you, Frank LaWall, that none of the Ayers will leave, if that is what you are hinting at!"

"Fires spread," said LaWall.

Young Max spoke. "You can't threaten us, mister cowman! We don't scare, savvy! My mother wouldn't let me take my rifle out of the house with me. But if I had it, I'd——"

Frank LaWall's .45 rose. The barrel crashed down on young Max's head. His knees buckled and he fell down the steps, his inert body stopping on the last step. Margaret screamed and Jennie's small face twisted with tears. Only Mrs. Ayers remained calm.

"Will you leave, please?"

"I could have killed him," growled LaWall.

"Maybe—he's dead!" cried Jennie.

Margaret sat down and held her brother's head on her thigh. The boy's thick hair was matting with blood. She put her hand inside his shirt and said, "His heart is beating, Jennie; he's only unconscious. Run to the well and pump some cold water, quick!"

Jennie grabbed a bucket and ran to the well. She pumped hurriedly, the squeaky cylinder sliding up and down in the rusty pipe. Margaret lowered her head and sobbed over her brother. Mrs. Ayers' dark eyes were bright with anger.

Jib Hobson said, "I'm sorry, ma'am."

She looked at him. "You're a killer, sir, or else you wouldn't ride with these gunmen."

Frank LaWall said, "Dusty, go back on the ridge. Watch the place with your rifle an' protect us as we ride out."

Jacobson turned his horse and rode up the slope where he went into the pines. Young Max stirred and Margaret helped him up. Half-carrying her brother, she got him inside; Jennie came with the bucket, the bottom covered with cold water. She stuck her tongue out at Frank LaWall.

"Let's go," said LaWall.

The cowman and Jib Hobson reined around and rode off. When the ridge hid them, Dusty Jacobson rode down, and joined them. Jacobson thought, *Well, what the hell . . . might just as well play the horse till his knees cave in. . . .* He looked at Frank LaWall and said, "Max Ayers might come a-huntin' you with a rifle or sixer when he hears about this, Frank."

"Let 'im come," grunted LaWall. He himself had not liked the idea of beating down the youth—he had thought of War Chief when he had struck. But it might bring about its results: it might be instrumental in driving the Ayers family out of Mad River, and that was what he wanted.

Jib Hobson was silent, and he did not like his thoughts. He remembered Mrs. Ayers, standing back there on the porch—she had been frightened and sick inside, yet her dark eyes had hidden this. She had looked at him, and that look and its meaning had hurt him more than he had liked . . . or cared to admit.

Hell of a role, he thought.

CHAPTER 14

BUCK MCKEE was squatted in the brush, talking with Ogo. The old squaw shaded her eyes with her seamed hand and her small eyes pulled even smaller in her wrinkled head. "Rider come to camp, McKee."

Buck nodded.

Five minutes later, when the rider was close enough for identification, Buck saw it was a girl, who rode a stout black workhorse. She clung to the saddle-horn and bounced with each jump of her heavy mount.

"Who is she, Ogo?"

Ogo shielded her eyes again. "Him Jennie Ayers," she said. "Him daughter Ayers. Papa work on dam."

Buck stepped out. He grabbed the big horse by the bridle and stopped him. The black was lathered with sweat. Jennie rode an old army saddle and she had a shotgun across the front of it.

"I'm Buck McKee. I guess you're Jennie Ayers."

"Daddy tol' me about you," said Jennie. "They—they hit my brother. They knocked him down an' his head bled."

"Who hit him?"

"Frank LaWall."

Buck finally got the story out of the little girl. Ogo came out of the brush, grinning toothlessly. "So LaWall hit kid, huh?"

Buck was silent. Jennie was weeping a little. Ogo said, "Don't cry, Jennie. Brother well soon. LaWall pay for that, too."

"I can't help cryin', Ogo."

Buck finally spoke. "You go back to the farm, Jennie. I'll tell your daddy. Did your mother send you here?"

"No, I sneaked out. I had to let daddy know. Mother is afraid that if dad found out—he might get a gun. But I wanted him to know, sir. If they come again——"

Buck glanced inquiringly at the squaw.

"You ride back home, honey," said the squaw. "McKee, him tell your dad. That best. You—your nerves worry. Bad."

Buck knew what Ogo meant. When Max Ayers heard of his son's beefing, the farmer would be mad, but if Buck told him he could sort of hold him down; on the other hand, with the story direct from his younger daughter's lips the effect on Ayers would be more bombastic.

"Do as Ogo says, Jennie."

"All right." The girl turned the big black. She rode off across the Basin floor. Buck scowled and thought. "This Ayers a hot-tempered gent, Ogo?"

"Him be mad."

Buck said, "You keep guard, woman." He got his horse from the high buckbrush and rode back to the dam on Wildcat Creek.

The walls on Sin Braden's tent were rolled up and Buck could see the woman's legs. He rode up close and dismounted. Sin was dobbing cold cream on her face.

"Good lord," groaned Buck, "don't try the impossible, woman!"

Sin turned, hand poised. She smiled. "Not to try to make an ol' hen purty, Buck; just to keep this wind an' dust from cuttin' my skin too much. Say, didn't I see a black horse down yonder on the Basin?"

Buck told her.

Hurriedly Sin Braden rubbed in the remainder of the cold cream. "We'll have to talk to Max," she declared. "Both of us better do it, Buck."

"After chuck."

Max Ayers came up to Buck. He was a wiry man. Back east, while in the steel mills, he had contracted a touch of tuberculosis, according to the doctors, but his four months in Arizona had evidently arrested the dreaded disease.

"Didn't Jennie ride into camp, McKee?"

Buck said, "Come over into Sin's tent," and Max Ayers followed him.

"You givin' me my time?" That was the standard joke in the camp. Nobody had ever been discharged; Sin Braden was that hard up for help. Not that there was ever reason to discharge a worker.

Sin was at the mess tent. She saw them and came over. Ayers wore a perplexed look. Buck told him about the girl's message. The thin man started from his stool in anger.

"Sit down, please, Max," said Sin Braden.

Buck was restless. He got to his feet. "Max, don't do anythin' like that; we know what you're thinkin'. LaWall would like to kill you; if he didn't, Dusty Jacobson would. Your boy is all right; he was only stunned. Just sit back, hold onto your impatience. Work with us, not against us."

"You've got a fine wife," put in Sin Braden, "an' a fine family. LaWall was tryin' to do two things: drive you from the Basin or make you fight. Do neither, an' when the time comes ripe, we'll either jail him or kill him."

"But if he comes back——"

"He won't come back. We're sure of that. He's got a big plan in the wind, and he won't bother you again. And if he does, the boy will be armed next time."

Ayers debated that, scholarly face serious. "All right," he finally said, "I'll be with you all the way, McKee. An' you, too, Sin. But I better go home an' see the boy, and spend the night with the missus and the children."

"That's a good plan," said Buck.

Ayers left to eat. Sin said, "His wife will talk him out of it completely, Buck. She's a level-headed, wonderful woman."

Buck went to the mess table where he sat next to Tortilla Joe. While the fat Mexican shovelled down beans and spuds, washing them on their way with hot coffee, Buck ate slowly, his mind running ahead. This was the night that Hans Sexton was to ride to the N Bar S.

"Thees work, she ees make me hongry *mucho*," said Tortilla Joe, biting into a huge *tortilla*, one of the last of the sackful given him by Peta Gomez. "When I run out of *tortillas*, I go ees an' veeseet weeth Peta."

"Franco'll stick you with his banana knife," said Buck.

"Putt, that beeg steef! He ees full of the hot air, nó?" But still, Tortilla Joe was scowling, dark forehead pulled down in thought.

Ayers rode out of camp. He lifted a hand to Buck and smiled. Buck and Tortilla Joe settled beside a rock up on the slope. There was some thick buckbrush behind them and Dondo's voice came from it.

"Tonight, Sexton go, huh?"

"Tonight's the night," affirmed Buck.

"I follow."

They heard the savage move back into the brush. Buck chewed on his toothpick and scowled. Tortilla Joe sucked on a cold horn-husk cigarette and regarded his thick knuckles as he thought.

"Later on," said Tortilla Joe, "we lower the single-tree on Hans Sexton, huh? We get heem with the goods, no?"

Buck drew his finger through the dust. "Good as any time," he agreed, "an' the proper time, I reckon, Sin an' me talked it over an' decided that tonight was the night. He's been spyin' in this camp long enough. Sin's jerked in all the workmen from the other dams an' has them here workin'. Remember when we rode into Mad River, when LaWall an' Jacobson hooly-hanned our broncs? Remember them dust spots we saw, one over each dam?"

"Yeah, I remember good."

"Sin tells me she had a few men at each dam, puttin' the finishin' touches on them. You know, a dam settles some, 'specially when made out of this 'dobe dirt. So these men—about two at a dam—have been puttin' a little extra dirt on each after the main crew had left."

"Where does that leave us, huh?"

"Well, as I said, Sin pulled these hands in. I got her to do it, Tortilla. For, with them in this camp, there are only guards on the dams—an' that is usually only one man, who stays there nights."

Tortilla Joe saw the light at last. "So you build thees trap, huh, an' you hope Frank LaWall, he heet at one of the dams, no? Hans Sexton, he breeng LaWall news, tell him no mens at dam. Then Jib Hobson, when he meet us at the beeg pine on the Skunk Creek, he tell us an' then we set trap, huh?"

"That's the way we see it, Tortilla."

They rolled cigarettes and smoked them. Gradually the dusk fell back and the night shadows reached slowly across the Arizona high country. Buck sat there and dwelt on the mysteries of night. He watched the shadows come in: there was a play of light against darkness, and the struggle was won by darkness.

He shifted position, ran over their position in his mind. He and Sin Braden had agreed on one thing: they would let Frank LaWall make the break, then they would step into the breach. This way, they would have the law on their side—not that Nappy Hale counted much, but the legality of the thing was what counted. And, secretly, Buck hoped LaWall would make that point soon.

He knew that the cowman would drive to a quick finish. For, with each passing day, the settlers, the farmers, were becoming more securely rooted into the Mad River soil. True, two farmers had left, driven out by fear of the N Bar S. But others would soon take their places: in fact, six families were to come in the next week. LaWall might win—but to do so he could not afford to dally.

Tortilla Joe looked up. He said, "There goes Hans Sexton, Buck." He cursed the dirt-man under his breath in rapid Spanish.

Sexton rode a dark brown horse. Buck noticed that the horse did not have white-stockings or a bald face. A horse marked by white legs and a white blaze in his forehead can easily attract attention in the dark when a black or sorrel could pass unseen. The farmer pointed the bronc toward his farm, hidden by the night down there on the sagebrush flats of Mad River.

"Actin' like he's headin' for home," said Buck. "Then, when he gets down below, an' when he gets outa sight, he'll swing aroun' an' head north, pushin' toward the N Bar S." He was heavy with an unseen weight.

"What we do with heem?"

"Do with him, Tortilla Joe? Well, here's the lay. Day after tomorrow, we pull out from this Wildcat Crick dam, pulling our horses an' outerfit further south. We settle on Willow Crick next, I think, accordin' to Sin Braden."

"Thees dam, she weel be feeneeshed by then?"

Buck nodded. "All except the facin' with stone an' the final work on the spillway. Reckon it must be all of ten miles from here to the site of the next dam. Of course, we leave guards here, though."

"Me, I do not follow you, *senor*."

Buck shrugged. "Maybe it won't work; maybe it will. Anyway, we aim to give it a whirl. Hans Sexton will tell Frank LaWall an' Jib Hobson will tell us." He fell to brooding again and then added, "I sure hope Jib don't mis-step, Tortilla Joe. Did you see Janice's eyes when she looked at him? They were like——" Buck wondered what words would fit.

"Peta's eyes, they light up too—like two coal-oil lamps." Tortilla Joe's choice of similes was severely limited. "But they are not for me; they have bad wicks—the light ees deem. Too much garlic."

Buck had to smile. He looked around, his hand on his gun, as Dondo came from the brush with, "Me, Buck." The half-naked little Apache squatted and said, "Sexton, him bein' followed. Pone."

Buck said, "Pone will watch him, huh?"

"Pone watch close."

"We'll get him," said Buck, "when he comes back, Dondo."

Dondo nodded. "Pone come in ahead of him. Him tell us."

They heard boots on the rocks below, then a heavy puffing as the thick figure of Sin Braden climbed into view. The husky woman, still puffing, sat down on a rock, and hugged Dondo, who giggled like a school-girl.

"That damned Sexton rode out, men. We'll get him when he comes back. Pone followin' him, Dondo?"

"Pone along, Sin."

Sin Braden tickled him. "You danged little heathen, why don't you put on some clothes, you red rascal. And what would Ogo say if she saw me with my arm aroun' you like this. She'd run me down with a butcher knife."

"I wouldn't let her."

Buck McKee smiled and relieved his inner tension.

CHAPTER 15

HANS SEXTON had no reason to believe that he was known at the dirt-camp, but caution rode always on the man's thick shoulders. He had done time at the state penitentiary in Indiana; had been pardoned two years before. His pardon read that, if he ran afoul of the law again, he would be returned to Indiana to complete the last ten years of a thirty year sentence for bank robbery. Only Hans Sexton, here in Arizona, knew about his pardon . . . and the twenty years he had served behind bars.

He had headed West, intending to hide his identity in the raw frontier. He had changed his name. The scar on his nose—the one he had received from a knife in a fellow criminal's grip—he said he had obtained in the Indian Wars. The only thing of shady character he had carried out since his pardon was his spying for Frank LaWall in the dirt-camp.

He rode east toward his farm. He had joined with LaWall because of the high wages: he was no farmer—when this was over, he would drift out. 'Frisco was still a wide-open town, although it was growing; Los Angeles was booming along. Yes, and there was Las Vegas, where gambling was legal; and Reno, where a man could pick a good living, they told him, by bucking the tiger in the gambling dens.

Before he got to the farm, though, he turned north. The night was dark and they could not see him from the

Wildcat Creek dam. He gave brief thought to Dondo and Pone and Ogo, and he felt a touch of uncertainty. Those Apaches could trail a man come high-water and mud.

Now he pushed his horse hard, a man who rode at a long lope, braced with his hands flat on his saddle-fork. This would be the last time: tomorrow he would be gone. He would get his wages tonight and drift, and he'd tell Frank LaWall that.

Pone did not follow him directly. The little Apache clung to the rim of the hills, his ear tuned to the night and its sounds.

Finally he was on the pine-studded hogback behind the N Bar S. He thonged a buckskin cord around his horse's jaws to stifle any desire to neigh. Then he lay on the ground, feeling vibrations in the earth that no white man could detect. Once he laid his head down, ear against the sod; he stayed that way some time, and then he smiled quickly. Hans Sexton had passed below him and was riding into the N Bar S.

He heard the guard say, "Who goes there?" The man's voice was sharp and that was why it penetrated the distance. He could not hear Sexton's reply. He saw the door to a cabin open and he saw Sexton against the lamplight before the door closed.

Frank LaWall was sitting on a rawhide-bottomed chair, sitting backwards with his legs around the uprights. He was scowling, his darkly handsome face showing displeasure. Jib Hobson lay on a bunk, his gun pulled up so he would not rest on it. That way, the .45 lay close to his hand. Dusty Jacobson squatted on the floor, his Colt moved ahead for comfort, and the dark man rubbed his sunken, broken face slowly with long fingers. Hans Sexton closed the door and said, "Well, I got here."

"Where t'hell were you the other night?" asked Frank LaWall shortly.

Hans Sexton sat on a chair. He leaned it back against the wall, resting the uprights solidly against the logs. He got his balance carefully. "Went to bed," he said. "Wanted things to look natural. Figured I'd sneak out later on an' ride over here but damn it, I was tired—and I went to sleep."

"What'd you figure I pay you wages for?"

"You didn't need me." Sexton spoke sharply. "And

by the way, when you mention wages—that reminds me, you owe me some dough, huh. Way I figure, about five hundred; ain't that right?"

"We'll get to that later."

Hans Sexton said, dangerously, "Not later—now, Frank."

Dusty Jacobson moved his heavy bulk. "The man wants his money, Frank," he said quietly. "Give it to him so we can get on with this talk. We ain't got all night. I've missed too much beauty sleep already." He yawned into his cupped hand.

"Settle up an' get on," growled Jib Hobson.

Frank LaWall said, "I can run this without your loop in it, Jib," and took out his wallet. The leather pouch was thick and Hans Sexton studied it with a covetous air. LaWall counted out five one-hundred dollar bills and tossed them to Sexton. Although the farmer had seen LaWall count them, he wet his dirty thumb and ran through the bills, counting aloud.

"He can add," said Dusty Jacobson, "an' he can count an' he takes no man's word. When you get a man like that, Jib, you got a fellow that can crawl purty low."

"Why tell me?" said Jib Hobson.

Dusty Jacobson held the youth's eyes squarely. "You're a young man, Jib, an' you'll find out you'll learn a lot by watchin' the other fellow. That way, if you watch enough, you can see into his character, his make-up. Men are like hosses after you've been aroun' them some time—only nice thing about a hoss, he can't talk." He yawned again.

"You lookin' for hell?" demanded Hans Sexton.

"Oh, no," said Jacobson, mockingly.

Hans Sexton thought about telling LaWall he was pulling out, then decided against it. He'd tell nobody—he'd just drift. And by the time the N Bar S boss found out he was gone, he'd be a thousand miles away. Sexton liked that thought: he was tired of Mad River Basin.

"Well, what's new?"

LaWall asked, "How did Max Ayers take the horntrimmin' I handed his kid, Hans?"

Sexton hid his surprise. "Never knew you bulldozed the kid, Frank. Not that he didn't need it, either. That reminds me, Max did leave camp tonight; early too. Maybe he went home, huh?"

"Never heard no talk about it in camp, huh?"

"Nary a thing. Though Jennie Ayers did come into camp, I reckon. Saw Max talkin' with Sin Braden an' McKee, then after chuck he got a hoss an' rid home. Me, I don't figure he'll make any fuss. Frank. You're too dangerous—an' you got two dangerous guns here." He glanced at Jib Hobson and Dusty Jacobson.

LaWall was silent for some time. "What's new at the dirt camp?"

Sexton bit off a chew of Star. He rolled the thick tobacco into his cheek, punched it three times rapidly with his teeth, then settled down to a slow, methodical chewing. He told them as to how the dam would be finished by tomorrow morning and that the dirt camp was moving south to work on Willow Creek. That would leave only old Smokey Platt at the Wildcat Creek dam as a guard. Later, of course, the finishers would come back, after the dam had settled, and face and surface the earth-fill blockade. But that would be a month away, anyway.

Frank LaWall's eyes were musing. He rubbed his hand through his red hair. "And what about the other dams, Hans?"

Sexton chewed diligently. "From what I make out, there's only goin' be a guard at each dam, accordin' to Sin Braden, 'cause she needs plenty of help buildin' this Willow Creek dam, seein' it won't be long until col' weather sets in, making the day short an' then there'll be some snow this winter, of course."

"That all you know, Sexton?"

Sexton grinned crookedly. "Ain't that enough, Frank?" He mentally reviewed the past events in the dirt camp and skimmed the cream off them and put them into words. "Of course, you know Tim Pinkey an' Nye Thorp got ascared, after you burned down Bill Dighton's, an' they pulled stakes. Oh, yes, Sin Braden said there was a bunch of new settlers comin' in, prob'ly next week. Accordin' to her, she had one of her surveyors lay out their homesteads down on the Basin an' they've already filed first papers in Wishbone at the court-house."

Dusty Jacobson smiled crookedly. "Day by day, they get a stronger and stronger hold, an' their roots get deeper an' deeper. . . ."

"They'll meet destruction when they get here," vowed

Frank LaWall. He got to his feet and put his hands behind his back. "They'll see a lot of burned homestead shacks, an' if that doesn't turn them back, *we'll turn* them back. 'Cause by next week this whole thing will be over. Either we'll win . . . or lose."

"Yeah?" Jib Hobson spoke.

"We hit Wildcat dam tomorrow night," said Frank LaWall. He drove one fist into the palm of his hand. "We hit it an' blow it skyhigh with powder an' if they come, it means a battle." He halted suddenly and looked at the door. Somebody was knocking lightly against it."

"Daddy, let me in."

The harshness left the big cowman's face. He opened the door. War Chief came in, dressed in a flannel nightgown. He wore moccasins. "I was going to bed, daddy, an' I had to say good night to you first."

Frank LaWall kissed him. He patted him on the back. "Now you run into bed, you little Indian."

War Chief said, "Good night, Dusty. Good night, Jib." He looked inquiringly at Hans Sexton. "What's your name?"

"Hans."

"I've never seen you before," said War Chief. "Good night, Hans."

When the boy was gone, Hans Sexton said, "Your boy, huh, Frank?"

Frank LaWall was himself again. "He called me *dad,* didn't he?" he snapped. . . . "Where were we—oh, yeah, I remember. We knock ol' Smokey Platt over an' plant dynamite an' lift that dirt to the clouds."

"It might be guarded," said Hans Sexton. "Of course, I understand not now, but McKee an' Sin Braden might change their minds. That old colonel—he's a-settin' over there givin' orders, his dead laig pushed out ahead of him——If he bit hisself he'd die of poison, sure as hell."

"No danger there?" asked LaWall.

"Nothin' besides his big mouth. He might talk a man to death, at that. Maybe he is dangerous if you're close enough." Hans Sexton allowed himself to smile. "I'll tell you what, Frank. We say they leave the dam heavily guarded. Then I meet you men in the pines back of the dam, up where Wildcat Crick enters the rocks. You know, about five miles above the dam."

"All right. An' if you're not there, we'll know the whole thing is okay. And remember I'm countin' on help from inside from you. You can unload shells an' jim up guns, an' things like that."

"I'll do that," promised Hans Sexton.

Jib Hobson had watched the scene through thoughtful eyes. He had the impression of something moving in this room, something nobody could see or feel or taste, and he knew it was his nerves. And with this he felt a sense of shame, for he was not proud of his role in this game of war; yet, he realized, he had played a needed part, for without him Sin Braden and Buck McKee and his fellow farmers would have had no inkling of the plans that were brewing on this dark night.

Frank LaWall looked at him. "What do you say, Jib?"

Hobson was silent, evidently thinking. "Sounds okay to me, Frank. Fact is, I don't see how it can miss . . . if that's what you want. . . ."

LaWall looked at Jacobson. The big man rubbed his broken, sunken cheek slowly. . . . "The iron fits good with my plan, Frank."

"That's it, then," declared LaWall.

Hans Sexton got to his feet. He ran his finger around his mouth, snagged his chewed tobacco, and flung it into the brass spittoon. He wiped his finger carefully on his dirty trousers. "I'll see you then, tomorrow."

Dusty Jacobson blew out the lamp. They went outside. Sexton mounted and turned his horse and rode out fast. Jacobson said, "Me for my bunk," and moved off into the darkness. Jib Hobson started off, too, and Frank LaWall said, "Jib, just a minute?" and his voice was low.

Jib Hobson stopped, heart beating heavily. Was the man suspicious? He stood there, looking at the red-headed man, and LaWall did not look at him; he stood looking at the mountain.

"What'd you want?"

Frank LaWall said, "There was a moon last night, wasn't there? I woke up once, and it was bright across my room. I wonder what time that was?"

"I couldn't sleep well," said Jib Hobson. "It came up about eleven." The tension had left him.

"Good night," said LaWall.

Jib Hobson murmured, "Good night," and went to the

bunkhouse. He could hear the hoofbeats of Hans Sexton's horse. Sexton rode fast, for he was in a hurry—he had a stout horse, a grain-fed bronc. Come daylight, he would have sixty miles between him and this range, and he would be across the *Sangre de Marias,* skirting the edges of the desert, riding through ocotillo and barrel cacti. He would hole up in Manzanita at noon, spend the hot part of the day there in *siesta,* and dusk would find him across the desert, with Nevada ahead and California to the south.

He followed a mountain trail, pounding along the dim path. His horse was sure-footed, a mountain horse. Pone followed him, moving on the ridges. Hans Sexton was heading for Wildcat Creek, but Pone did not know until later that Sexton would not ride into the camp. Eight miles above the camp, the man swung on the north fork, heading into the mountains.

Pone listened, marked his position. There was something wrong here. He fingered the long knife in his belt, then thought better of it. He would get to Buck McKee and tell him.

He rode fast, bronc running through the night. He perched on the broad back, clinging to the horse's mane, and he beat him with the free end of the rope that he used for a bridle.

CHAPTER 16

BUCK AND DONDO squatted in the brush. A shambling form came closer, crashing through the rosebushes, and Buck thought first it was a bear, until he saw that a bear was not that tall.

"She ees me, Tortilla Joe."

Buck smiled. "This way, Tortilla."

Tortilla Joe turned and came and squatted beside them, puffing from his exertions. "You hombres find swell hidin' places. You are hard to fin' in the dark, no?" He looked at Buck, then at the silent Apache. "What you wait for, huh?"

"Pone," grunted Dondo.

"Oh, *si*, heem follow Sexton, huh?"

Dondo brought his head up. "Rider is come, Buck."

At first, Buck could hear nothing more than the chirp of a cricket and Tortilla Joe's snores. He jabbed his elbow into the Mexican's ribs. "Shut up an' listen." With that noise gone, he heard a horse in the distance, running toward them with the sound of his hoofs beating stronger.

"Pone," said Dondo.

Buck frowned. "Wonder where Sexton is?"

"Maybe he ride aroun', maybe Pone take short cut."

Fifty feet away, the Apache left his horse, and ran toward them. He said, "Dondo, Buck; *donde estas?* Where you at?" Buck called to him and the Apache found them. He spoke in rapid monosyllables.

"Sexton, him go N Bar S. Him talk, LaWall. Sexton, him leave. Him ride this way; him swing north. Him go over mountains, free."

Buck growled, "Pullin' out on us, huh?"

"We fix him," said Dondo.

Tortilla Joe shrugged. "Why not let heem go, Buck? What he knows, we can hear from Jib Hobson."

Buck said, "The dirty traitor! Stay in our camp, learn our plans—then pull out when the goin' got tough, figurin' we didn't know about his dirty tricks. No siree, we'll run him out—he can't get out without payin'!"

"Me say same," declared Dondo.

Buck and Dondo had their horses tied in the rocks. They ran to them, hit their saddles. Dondo rode an old army saddle, no bigger than a postage stamp—or any more comfortable. Tortilla Joe had his horse at the camp. He ran through the night, ambling heavily along. Colonel Henry S. Braden came out of the mess tent after a midnight snack. Tortilla Joe ran into him, knocking him one way and his crutches the other. The colonel hollered and sat down.

"Oh, my broken leg—Tortilla, you clumsy ox, I'll bust —Hey, cook, help me up, this Mexican——"

"You go to hell," said Tortilla Joe. He was slinging his kak on his bronc. He reached under, grabbed the cinch, pulled it around and threaded his latigo strap through the ring. He pulled it tight, tied the knot. "You can help heem, cook."

"Don't know whether he's worth it," said the cook. He stood, arms akimbo, looking down at the fuming colonel. Tortilla Joe found his stirrup and went up, loping away and leaving them standing like that.

Pone had a fresh horse. Tortilla Joe met the three riders in the creek bottom; they headed north fast. Pone, perched on his fresh mount, rode with his rope flailing his bronc.

Dondo and Pone were keeping up an excited jabber, the most Buck had ever heard them talk. And, because he knew a little Apache, he could tell that Pone was telling his brother the approximate location of Hans Sexton. They came to a grassy mesa and here Dondo took the lead.

Pone looked back. "We get there, soon, Buck."

Buck grunted, "Danged near time, Pone." Catclaw had stung him across the right cheek, drawing a little blood. Besides, his face didn't feel any too well; the blows of Dusty Jacobson had not lost their sting, yet.

"My horse, she ees winded," grunted Tortilla Joe.

"Two miles," declared Pone.

They followed the mesa trail, swinging around sandstone rocks, and then suddenly, without warning, they were on the edge of a wide mountain road, hacked through pine and spruce. The wind was cold here, whipping down from the snow, and Buck wished he had another coat, despite the heat that excitement was sending through his veins.

"Road—go to Manzanita," explained Dondo. "Years ago, men build. No use now." He left his horse and ran to the trail and knelt beside Pone, who was on his knees. Buck let his reins fall and he stepped down. Tortilla Joe followed him and they looked at the trail, studying the tracks there. Pone mumbled, "Bear track, elk track. Him track deer. Horse there."

"No Sexton horse," said Dondo. "Sexton horse no come yet. No other way, Pone?"

Pone's beady eyes were bright marbles as he considered this alternative. "He come this way, Dondo. Him in hurry. This shortest way. Him come."

Dondo straightened. "We wait, men."

They hid their horses in the brush. Then they squatted

there, all hidden; they watched the moonlit trail. Twenty minutes later Dondo said, "Rider come, horse trot."

Pone listened. "That him, Buck."

Buck drew his plan up hurriedly. The two Apaches and Tortilla Joe were to squat in the brush, rifles ready. He would go into the trail and stop Hans Sexton. But, if the man was riding too fast, and Buck could not grasp his bridle reins and stop his horse, they were to shoot the bronc out from under the traitor.

Dondo cocked his head. "Horse come at trot only."

Buck crossed the strip and leaned against the opposite bank. When Hans Sexton came around the curve he would not see the tall cowboy until he was right on him. True to Dondo's prediction, Sexton's horse came at a trot. The long, hard ride, coupled with the steepness of the mountain pass, had slowed the animal to a long trot. Now Sexton rode around the bend and now Buck stepped out, grabbing the horse by the bridle reins, and jerking the beast to a sliding halt.

The unexpected appearance of Buck McKee brought a gasp to the traitor's lips. "McKee——?" He couldn't believe his eyes. McKee was supposed to be in camp, some fifteen miles to the south, and here—Sexton reached for his gun, got his hand on the holstered weapon, then halted as Tortilla Joe, accompanied by Dondo and Pone, came out of the brush, rifle raised.

"Your gon—you forget him, no?" commanded the Mexican.

Sexton took his hand back. Buck got the man's gun. He said, "Get off that horse, you damned traitor! We knew all about you when you were in camp! We just let you go on double-crossin' us because we figured it wouldn't hurt us, seein' we know all that happens on the N Bar S! Get off that bronc, I tell you!"

Sexton's eyes showed fear. He made no move toward dismounting. Buck planted his feet wide, dug in his bootheels, grabbed Sexton by the right arm, and dragged him from leather.

Sexton landed hard on the rocky soil.

Buck stepped back. He handed his gun and belt to Tortilla Joe. "Neither of us has a gun, Sexton," he said stoutly. "Step up on your feet, an' get the worst whuppin' a man ever got!"

But when Sexton got up, he had his jack-knife in his hand. The spring blade shot open, he lunged. The blade reflected moonlight. Buck saw the reflection and jumped to one side. He twisted, the knife came down; the cowpuncher kicked Sexton in the belly, doubling him. He got the man's wrist in both hands and bent the arm back, the knife pointing harmlessly upward.

Buck's blood was cold. He had seen, and used, cold steel during the war, and the thought of it sent ice-water in his veins. Dazed, breathing heavily, Sexton fought to hang onto the knife. But Buck's strength was too much; the knife fell to the ground. Dondo darted in and picked it up.

"I keep heem, Buck."

Dondo got hurriedly out of the way. Angered, his breath back now, Hans Sexton rushed, arms working hard. Buck side-stepped, hit him twice, straightened him. They were hard blows, and Sexton felt their power. A mauling fist crashed against the side of Buck's head. Buck went forward, fists working savagely, and Sexton gave ground. Buck found his opening and knocked the man down.

"You talkin'?" he gritted.

Sexton sat there, spitting blood. He mumbled, "To hell with you, McKee. If you want to find out anythin', you're workin' over the wrong man!"

Buck read stubbornness in the stolid man's voice. He wiped the blood from his mouth. Sexton was blubbering, his face beaten and cut. One eye was swelling shut; the other was cut. His fight was gone, yet he was stubborn. Buck moved forward, intending to pull the man up, and beat him down again. But Dondo stepped in, pushed him back.

"Pone an' me, we make him talk."

Buck said, "All right, Dondo."

Naked fear was quick in Hans Sexton's eyes. "Don't turn me over to these savages, McKee!"

"What did you cook up at LaWall's tonight?"

Sexton eyed him. "Why not ask your spy, Dusty Jacobson? He is Dusty Jacobson, ain't he?"

Buck nodded. "We'll see him, later." Sexton might just

as well think Jacobson was the spy, not Jib Hobson. "But we want your story, now."

Still Sexton was stubborn. Not that he wanted to shield Frank LaWall; he was done with him. But some inner stubbornness, some obstinate trait in his surly nature, made him rebel against releasing any information. "You go to hell an' stay there, McKee."

Buck stepped back. "Go to work, Apaches," he said.

Terrified, Hans Sexton tried to get up. But Dondo's long knife, pressed against his throat handle-first, forced him back in a lying position. Suddenly Dondo reversed the knife, pointing the sharp point against the man's throat.

"I cut him," he grunted.

Sexton screamed. Buck grinned, knowing the savage was just scaring the man. Pone came close, knife sharp. The blade descended, slitting Sexton's sleeve like it were paper.

"Open up vein," grunted Pone.

He turned his knife, putting the edge against the man's hairy forearm. The skin broke open a little under the razor edge. Sexton screamed, "I'll talk, McKee. Get these damned Injuns off me, pronto!"

Buck said, "Step back, boys," and the two Apaches moved off, grinning. Sexton stared at the drops of blood along his arm. "They aim to hit Wildcat Dam tomorrow night—after you people pull out your rigs an' outfits. With only the ol' guard there, they aim to blow the whole dam skyhigh. That's the whole story, Buck."

Buck was silent for a long moment. Then he said, "All right, Sexton, get on your horse an' get over the mountains. An' never come back to Mad River again, *sabe?*"

"I'm not plumb loco," growled Sexton.

Tortilla had unloaded the man's Colt. Now the Mexican tossed him the pistol. Sexton caught it, holstered it, climbed on his horse. He wrapped his quirt around the bronc's barrel and left in a scatteration of gravel and dust that hung on the moonlight. They listened to his hoofs run out into the distance.

"He don't like us," said Buck, grinning.

CHAPTER 17

THEY SQUATTED there, dark under the brittle moonlight, and built plans for the future. Janice Braden was in Buck's thoughts and the vision of her was brought by the memory of Jib Hobson. Hobson was in the N Bar S camp, and he occupied the same position that Hans Sexton had held in the dirt camp—if Hobson were caught, LaWall and Dusty Jacobson would kill him.

"We go warn Hobson, then?" asked Tortilla Joe.

Dondo and Pone were quiet, their dark eyes sharp. Buck spoke slowly. "The way I look at it, men, there's no use of Jib ridin' to the lone pine on Skunk Crick. We already know what Frank LaWall intends to do. And if Jib stays in camp, LaWall will have less chance of findin' out Jib is spyin' for us. Therefore, his neck is much safer."

Dondo said, "But Jib can't go, Buck. He do that, LaWall change plans."

Buck poked a rock with his fingers, moving it through the loose earth. "That's right, Dondo. If Jib left the N Bar S, then LaWall would be suspicious—he might change his plans, figurin' Jib had talked to us. And he prob'ly wouldn't hit the dam. We want him to do that, 'cause we'll stop him then and there . . . an' this war'll be a thing of the past."

Tortilla Joe rubbed his jaw thoughtfully. "Then, the ways I see eet, ees thees ways, Buck. We get word to Jeeb; he not meet you on Skunk Creek, no? He stay in camp, ride with LaWall tomorrow night. Then, right before fight, he sneak off—he come to us, an' then we go to troubles, no?"

Buck nodded. "That's it, Tortilla."

Pone spoke suddenly. "I go to N Bar S. I know how to reach Jib. I tell him. Tell him we know."

"I go with him," said Dondo.

Buck said, "Now wait a minute, fellows, this is our

job, too. You two boys aren't carryin' this fight alone, believe you me. Me an' Tortilla Joe got our fangs into this, an' we aim to fight it through."

Pone smiled slowly. The wrinkles broke across his leathery face. "White man, him loud. Him make much loud. Red man, him quiet. Me, Dondo, get work. We work pairs. One behin' other, coverin' other's trail."

"You go camp," declared Dondo. "Get camp ready to move. Make everythin' look right. Get men ready. Me, Pone tell Jib, no?"

Buck considered that. He did not want to make it look like the two pygmy Apaches were doing more than their share, nor did he like to have them ride on such a dangerous mission.

"All right, hombres."

They rode ten miles together until they came to the fork. Here one canyon went east, the other south. Buck and Tortilla Joe took the south turn, for it went to the Wildcat Dam. They had ridden the ten miles slow, letting their broncs gather some spent strength, for the ride out had drawn the edges from their mounts. And Dondo and Pone, if they ran into any trouble, would need fast, tough horses.

Once Buck and Tortilla Joe saw the two Apaches again. They were a mile or so north-east, moving across a rocky ridge. Pone and Dondo had ridden many times on dangerous missions. Therefore, they worked it easily, one hanging to a higher vantage than the other. This way, the upper Apache covered the lower one's advance, seeing any movement that escaped the other.

Their horses, wiry Indian ponies, were sure-footed and knew the brush. And when it was dangerous to stay on horseback, the Apaches would take to the dirt, moving ahead on foot.

The night was far spent when Pone reached the pines on the slope above the N Bar S ranch. Below him, sleeping on the moon-lit plateau, were the scattered buildings of the cow-outfit. He stood for a moment at the head of his sweaty pony, looking upward at the higher ridges. Somewhere Dondo ranged those higher points. Pone did not know that Frank LaWall was up there, too, hidden in the boulders.

For on this night, the big red-headed cowman had not

been able to sleep. Tomorrow night would either see him boss of Mad River range or see him broken.

He had dressed and gone into War Chief's room. He had stood by his son's bed, looking down at him. War Chief slept the deep untroubled sleep of childhood. He slept on his side, one arm under him and his right hand close to the big teddy-bear that he always took to bed with him.

His squaw said, "Is that you, Frank?"

He went to her room and looked in. "Yes. And how are you?"

She was silent for five seconds. Then she said, "I'd better go to the mission soon, Frank. I don't think it will be long now, and I want Father O'Flannigan to help me with my childbirth."

He said, "Day after tomorrow, we'll take you in. I couldn't sleep. I guess I'll go for a walk."

She knew him well. "Why can't you sleep? What's botherin' you?"

"Nothin'."

He went out into the crisp night air. The ranch lay in silent splendor. One of his dogs started barking and he silenced him angrily. The dog ceased. He had four of the brutes; big hounds that made savage watchdogs. They were better than human guards; they never slept at night.

He walked up the mountain, the tang of pine and spruce in his nostrils, and he found the old flat spot among the rocks. He squatted here with his back to a sandstone and looked across the moon-washed ridges of Mad River Basin. He did not see Pone move in, for Pone moved too quickly and too cleverly; he did not see Dondo, for Dondo was back of him—and the rocks behind him hid him from Dondo, hunkered on the high hill.

Had Frank LaWall moved, Dondo would have seen him—but the N Bar S owner sat silent, facing his thoughts and busy with them. Pone went through the buckbrush. He saw one of the dogs, curled beside the bunkhouse. His knife out, he went around the corner. Suddenly the cur sniffed him. He rose slowly, hackles rising. Pone's knife rose and fell and when it came back up, the sheen of the moonlight on it did not show. The dog lay with his throat cut.

Pone went along the bunkhouse wall. He came to the

window by Jib Hobson's bunk. Hobson lay on his back, snoring softly. Pone put his hand over the man's mouth and put his head close to Hobson's ear. He whispered, "Pone, Jib, Pone," and he held Hobson's mouth until sleep had left the man and sanity had him. "You hear me, Hobson?"

Hobson nodded.

Pone took his hand back. Squatted there, talking in short, terse sentences, he told about Hans Sexton, how he had come to tell him that Buck McKee and the dirtmen would be ready when the N Bar S hit at Wildcat Dam.

"No meet Buck on Skunk Crick."

Hobson nodded. "I'll ride with LaWall," he said quietly, whispering. "Then, right out of the coulee aways, I'll duck back into the brush. I'll be on your side then when the fightin' really starts."

Pone nodded. "I tell you, Jib." He was gliding away then, stepping over the dead hound. He halted at the edge of the building, small in the shadows, and then darted across the clearing. Frank LaWall, watching idly from the hilltop, saw him then.

He thought, at first, that the little Apache was a dog, the distance was so far and the moonlight so deceptive. Then his eyes told him it was either Pone or Dondo. His first thought was that the Apache had come to set fire to the N Bar S.

Then, when he saw no smoke, he gave that idea up. He silently cursed his dogs. The Apache, he figured, had just sneaked into camp to look around—he heard they did that some times. He silently jacked a cartridge into the barrel of his .25-35 Winchester rifle and waited.

Pone reached the edge of the brush, moved into that. Still Frank LaWall waited, for he knew the Apache would pass under him there in that treeless park. And when Pone did, he was on horse. Slowly the N Bar S boss raised his rifle and found the sight as best he could in the moonlight.

He followed Pone's progress across the strip. Once rosebushes shielded the Apache; LaWall moved his gun ahead, picked the little man up again. And when Pone was about five feet from the brush, Frank LaWall led him a little, squeezed his trigger, and shot twice.

The first bullet hit Pone in the chest. Had LaWall been shooting a soft-nosed shell, he'd have torn the Apache in two—but he shot a steel-jacketed bullet. As it was, the bullet almost knocked Pone from his horse. The second missed. It hit a rock and sang off across Mad River Basin.

Pone's terrified horse jumped into the high brush, the Apache hanging to his mane. The roar of the rifle beat across the stillness. LaWall never got to shoot again—the brush hid the wounded Indian. LaWall lowered his rifle, cursing a little. He wondered if he had hit the Apache. He had not been able to tell in the distance and the deceptive light.

Terrified, Dondo had heard the rifle reports, saw Pone flinch on his horse. But, because of the rocks, he had not been able to see Frank LaWall. Two desires tore at his wiry body: he wanted to get at LaWall and he wanted to get to Pone. The latter, he decided, would be the most important. Perhaps even now his brother was dying. Nevertheless the pygmy Apache sent four rifle bullets beating on the rocks that sheltered the gunman, for he had no way of knowing that Frank LaWall had been doing the shooting.

The bullets ricocheted from the rocks and sped off into distance to die. For the first time, Frank LaWall knew that a rifleman was above him, and he pulled back under the overthrust and lay down in the dark.

But in his haste to get to Pone, Dondo did not have time to fire again at Frank LaWall. Somewhere over him, the cowman heard a horse crash through the brush, but he could not see the rider. And, what was more, he wasn't going out looking for him. One of the Apaches could come silently behind him and cut his throat with a knife. His only chance was to keep his back to the rock and watch the clearing in front of him.

Dondo caught Pone a mile away. He grabbed him and said, "You shot, brother?" He stopped Pone's horse.

"No get off horse," said Pone slowly. "Never got back on. Look at wound, now? Bullet hit me in chest."

"Who shoot you?"

"Frank LaWall. I tell by his rifle sound. I know that rifle too well. I bleed, Dondo."

Dondo got some grass, matted it, and wiped the blood from Pone's chest. The bullet hole was high on his right side. He glanced at it and plugged it with grass and stopped the bleeding somewhat there. The bullet had passed right through, breaking the collar-bone as it came out, for Pone's shoulder sagged. Dondo cleaned this too, using another mop of grass; he plugged this, too.

"You make it to camp, Pone?"

"I go."

Dondo's voice held concern. "I leave you here. You keep rifle. LaWall no come. I get Ogo. Her fix you."

"I ride camp."

Dondo turned his horse loose. He got on Pone's bronc, sitting behind his brother. He got both arms around the sagging little man and held him. He put the horse ahead, letting him head toward the Wildcat Dam, and his own horse followed them—the single bridle-rein wrapped around his scrawny neck.

They had to move slowly. For, if the horse trotted or loped, the wound would start bleeding again. Dondo knew that Pone would live if he could conserve his blood, keep his blood in his body. Blood, to the Apaches, was the source, the center of life, and Dondo knew that Pone's strength lay in the dark fluid.

A terrible hate lay like a coiled snake in Dondo's breast. He blamed himself for the accident: he had not ridden close enough guard for his brother. This hate coiled and uncoiled in him. His bronze face was graven and seemingly without thoughts.

He said, "You feel fine, Pone?"

"I sick, Dondo."

Dondo rode for five miles or so in silence. He held his brother with one arm, with the other he guided the pony. Blood was oozing out of the wounds and he held the rough blockade in the front wound with his free hand. He could feel the sticky blood on his fingers. He pushed his chest against the matted grass on Pone's back. He could feel blood there, too.

Minutes stretched out, became hours. They moved slowly, winding along the base of mountains, seeking the level trails. Many times Dondo put the pony around longer paths, seeking to save his brother from bumping caused by the shorter, rockier trail. An icy chill came down from the snow. The night was running out of time.

Dondo said, "Ogo fix you, brother. Ogo fix you." That

was the one thought: Ogo, with her primitive skills, her calmness. He put the other into words. "The next time I met Frank LaWall, I kill him for this."

Pone smiled. "You no kill him, I will."

CHAPTER 18

WHEN BUCK MCKEE and Tortilla Joe came into the Wildcat Dam camp, Sin Braden was on guard with Ogo, and she came out of the brush carrying her Winchester. Buck pulled in his sweaty horse and looked at the squat, ungainly woman dressed in levis and a flannel shirt, her battered hat held to her rolled-up hair by a long hatpin.

"You're up late, Sin," he said, jokingly.

"When you buck a man like Frank LaWall, you have to stay awake late. Now what're you two hellions battin' aroun' the country for at this hour of the mornin'?"

Buck told her about Hans Sexton.

Sin Braden's seamed eyes grew reflective. "So Dondo an' Pone rode over to tell Jib, huh? Well, you better get some shut-eye, you two; mornin's right aroun' the bend, an' we start moving pronto at daybreak."

Tortilla Joe went right to sleep. Buck lay there between his sougans and dozed. Finally he too went to sleep. He was awakened by somebody shaking him vigorously. He looked sleepily into Sin Braden's wrinkled face.

"Dondo an' Pone, Buck—they haven't come back to camp yet, an' they should be here by now."

"What time is it?"

"Almost four."

Buck pulled on his boots, his spurs, and donned his Stetson and he was dressed. Tortilla Joe had come awake. He had lain there and listened to Sin's words. His brown eyes showed his alarm.

"We go look for them, Seen."

They got fresh horses and they headed out. Ogo stood and watched them go, her small face torn by conflicting emotions, chief of these being fear for the safety of her husband and brother-in-law. Her two daughters, Pipo and Nono, were settled across the brush, also keeping watch. Buck felt a pull of thankfulness. They were lucky to have such good guards as the Ilaks.

But mingled with this was a fear—a fear for Pone and Dondo. Had something gone wrong at the N Bar S? Surely something must have gone amiss; otherwise the Ilaks would be back into camp by now. They headed at a long trot for the cow-ranch.

The Mexican stifled a yawn behind a dirty palm. "All the time, there ees thees night riding, Buck, an' me for two are gettin' tired of eet. Now, when we get down in ol' Mejico, ees Santa Margarita——"

"We *siesta* about a week, maybe not that long. Then, you'll want to go some place else, and we'll be on our way."

Tortilla Joe grinned. "But eet weel be a rest, no?" Suddenly he pulled in his horse. "*Holla,* what ees that, huh? She ees Pone an' Dondo, no?"

The two Apaches were riding around a bend ahead. And Buck McKee, spurring his horse forward to meet them, took in their situation at a glance. He pulled in and Dondo raised his tired head.

"Pone, he ees shot." He spilled his story in rough English, rougher Spanish, and liquid Apache. Although Buck did not catch all of it, he understood enough. And his gaunt face was graven with his thoughts. Tortilla Joe crossed himself and said a little prayer under his breath. This done, he gave his thoughts and his deeds to the living and the wounded.

"We five, six miles from camp," he said. "We got to take Pone there, or Ogo here. Which do you say ees the best plan, Buck?"

"Go get Ogo."

Tortilla Joe turned his bronc, rearing the animal and lifting him around on the mountain trail. Then he was off, rocks lifting behind him; he went around the bend, and then Buck and Dondo heard only the dying sounds of his hoofbeats.

Buck dismounted and held Pone while Dondo got to the ground. Pone was smiling, a little too tightly, Buck figured. The game little Indian was holding his pain stoically. With Dondo's help, Buck got Pone from the tired horse, and he carried him to a grassy-spot under an overthrust of igneous boulder. There he lay him down and knelt beside him.

"You stopped most of the bleedin', Dondo. Now, if we can keep him comfortable until Ogo comes. You want some water, Pone?"

"Me take, water."

Buck untied his canvas water-bag from his saddle and put it to Pone's dry lips; the man drank eagerly. His thirst quenched, Pone lay back on the rock that Dondo had placed for a pillow and closed his eyes. His chest rose and fell to his measured breathing.

"You sure Frank LaWall did it?" asked Buck.

Dondo said, "I sure, Buck."

Buck mused. "Odd that he'd be up that time of the night."

"Sometimes him can't sleep. See him before at night. This time him hide too well. Dondo shot, could not hit."

The Indian put his back against a rock and closed his eyes. By now, all the sleep had left Buck. And inwardly he wrestled with his new angle to this predicament. He blamed himself for placing Pone in a position where Frank LaWall could shoot at him. He told Dondo this.

"Not your fault, Buck. You our friend. Pone do anythin' for you. Dondo do like, too. Just what you call it——?" He waved his hands rapidly. Buck understood that he meant: Fate did it, that's all.

"He'll come through," said Buck.

"Ogo make him live. Her fingers have magic." His voice, Buck noticed, held faith in it—faith for his squaw's logic of herbs and medicinal roots.

They hunkered there . . . and Buck thought of the night ahead. And he hoped that Frank LaWall would storm the dam. That meant, of course, that shooting would occur; this could be accompanied by bloodshed and bloodshed's accomplice, death. But it was better to get it over with and be done with it. The big cowpuncher had little fear. He had lost all his fear, it seemed, at San Juan and in the Philippines.

"They come," said Dondo.

Buck heard nothing. But he listened and then, in a few minutes, he heard approaching hoofs. Ogo rode a blue-roan mare; a thin beast but a tough animal. She carried a sack with her, holding it as she rode bareback.

Buck took the sack as she dismounted. He handed it to her then and she went to Pone, who opened his eyes and smiled at her. Then, suddenly, the small Indian twisted with pain, rolled half-way over, then fell back limp. Tortilla Joe took off his high-crowned hat and held it respectfully against his chest.

"You dang fool," ground out Buck; "he ain't dead—his chest is still risin'."

Tortilla Joe replaced his limp hat.

Carefully Ogo studied Pone's wound. Finally, her inspection done, she got to her feet, talking in Ilak Apache to Dondo, who nodded silently. Buck could not understand what she said because she talked too fast.

"She take Pone back to mountains," explained Dondo. "Herb there she need. I help her take him. She stay with him until well. You move camp today, huh?"

Buck said, "Yes."

"I come back aroun' time when sun stay there." He pointed straight up. Buck spoke to Pone. "You get well, fellow."

"I get well. Ogo make me well."

Buck had the impression that they wanted him and Tortilla Joe to leave.

They would take the wounded man back to the secret rendezvous deep in the *Sangre de Marias*. He and Tortilla mounted and rode to camp. They got there just as the cook was beating his triangle.

Pipo and Sin Braden met them as they rode in. Pipo was about seventeen, a thin, shy Apache. Sin asked hoarsely how Pone was getting along and Buck told her that Ogo was taking him back into the mountains.

"I was with Ogo when Joe came for her," said Sin huskily. "Well, them heathens'll fix him up. I've already told the men—most of them are mad enough to ride over to the N Bar S an' tackle it. That is, I only tol' them about Pone bein' shot, not about tonight."

Buck nodded. "That was all right, Sin. I'll tell them about LaWall's plan—tell them at chuck this mornin'."

Dirt men were filing into the mess tent. Tin plates and spoons were clattering. Buck and Tortilla Joe took a bench at the far end. Buck waited until some of the men had finished and were starting to leave the tent. He got to his feet and beat on the bottom of a tin plate with his fork. "Sit down, men, I've got somethin' to say."

Talking firmly, Buck told them what had happened: how Hans Sexton had been a traitor in the camp, how he and Tortilla Joe had cornered Sexton and made him talk, thereby revealing Frank LaWall's plan to blow up the Wildcat dam that night. He did not mention Jib Hobson's part as a spy in the N Bar S camp. He and Sin and Tortilla Joe and Janice and the Apaches had agreed to keep that secret.

"What do we do, Buck?" demanded Bill Dighton. "We goin' sit an' knit us some winter underwear while our dam goes sky-high?"

The dirt men and farmers talked this over angrily, and Buck let the rumble grow. Then he held up his hand and beat on the plate again until the men were silent.

"No, we won't be knittin' underwear, men." He outlined the plan to them. They would move, of course. Frank LaWall would have spies watching them, no doubt. But they could have guards stationed, too. The best thing was to let the spies alone, make everything look natural, and let the spies bring this information back to Frank LaWall.

"We'll move to our new site," said Buck. "Then, when dark comes, we sneak back here, under cover of night. We station out our men an' set a trap for the N Bar S. When they come in, we finish this trouble."

There was a short silence. Men peered into the future and tried to determine what was in store for them. Perhaps some of them would die this night. Finally Dirty Henry Smutton spoke.

"But what if they don't hit at the dam, Buck? What if they do like they did the time they were goin' burn down my house, an' they burned down Bill Dighton's?"

"That's a chance we'll have to take," said Buck. "The N Bar S, as close as Dondo can estimate, has about twelve riders, not countin' LaWall an' Jacobson. We've got to pull in some of our guards to equal that number of men."

"Take the guards off the dams we've built?"

"No, pull guards away from your homes."

They considered that. Max Ayres got to his feet. "We think that would be right, Buck—our women an' kids can guard our homes. But what if LaWall hits another dam, not Wildcat?"

Buck pondered over that. "Another chance we'll have to take, Max. But we got two guards on each dam. If somethin' does happen, at least one of them should get to us, tell us. Then, if the N Bar S does hit another dam beside Wildcat, we run them down an' fight it out, either in the mountains or the N Bar S home-camp."

"That's the talk," growled Len Carter.

Sin Braden took the floor. Cursing now and then, she reiterated what Buck had said. They'd come in at dark, take their positions in the brush, then wait for the N Bar S *skunks,* as she labeled them. Colonel Henry S. Braden beamed his satisfaction. He got to his feet and held his cup of coffee high.

"A toast, men, to the fight tonight."

"With you sittin' a mile behin' the dam out of gunrange," growled a bearded dirt-man. "No, siree, colonel, I don't drink. This is too serious."

"Me, neither," snapped another.

"Sit down, you ol' billy goat!"

The colonel blustered, the rope-like vein swelling on his forehead. He slammed his coffee cup down and spilled the liquid all over the front of his shirt and pants. "Mutiny," he stormed.

"Take eet easy," advised Tortilla Joe.

Buck spoke again. "If there are any of you who don't want to fight, you can stay in camp tonight. As I tol' you, Hans Sexton worked for Frank LaWall—we don't think there is another spy in this group. But we're goin' make sure that nobody rides out an' warns LaWall. There will be guards out all day and any man makin' a move to ride toward the N Bar S gets dragged into camp an' tried by a jury for treason."

"And hanged by his neck," added the colonel savagely.

"Shut up," growled Tortilla Joe, "or we'll hang you."

Buck asked, "Are there any questions?"

Evidently there were none. The men filed out. "We're on the right track now," growled one.

"We'll settle this for once an' for always."

Tents were coming down, being folded and put into wagons. Horses and mules were hitched to rigs instead of to fresnos and ploughs.

By mid-forenoon they had the wagons rolling toward the south and the site of the next dam.

The wagons were strung out in a long line, dust rising lazily from their wheels. Buck rode back and checked the Wildcat site. He sat his bronc and slowly ran his gaze across the dam and its surrounding. He built a mental picture of it for use that night. He knew the exact location of each clump of brush and each sizeable boulder. Tortilla Joe came riding out of the hills.

"Me, I ees talk with Peepo, Buck. She ees say that already there are LaWall spies, back een the heels."

Buck nodded. "Just leave them be," he said.

He and his Mexican partner rode to where the wagons toiled across the plain. Sin Braden rode back. "Some of the wagons are already unloadin', Buck. You should see the colonel! He's over there givin' orders, but Jens Jones is unloadin' where he wants—disregardin' the colonel entirely. How long have you known the ol' goat?"

"Too long," grunted Buck.

Tortilla Joe nodded. "And, never, een that time, has he run out of wind, Seen. Ah, eef we could only hook heem up to a windmill, no?"

The Latin sighed.

With Ogo leading the pony bearing the wounded Pone, the three Apaches went deep into the *Sangra de Maria* mountains, with Dondo following behind. Pone was silent as he rode, and his eyes were beady with illness. Hours later, when the sun was almost noon-high, they came to the canyon that Ogo wanted to reach.

"This is the spot, Dondo."

They had been silent for the most part on the inward trek. Now, working together, they loosened their tongues, casting off the silence they inevitably wore when around white men. Here tall palms almost filled a wild basin that had pools of water surrounded by tall green grass and rushes. Here a man could stand on the rocks and look across the limitless desert to the west.

Ogo went to the water and dug in the mud. She came back with a dark yellow clay. "This is the place, Dondo."

"You have enough to eat?" asked Dondo.

The squaw laughed. "Me, starve in this region!" she said in Apache. She pointed to the dates that hung in clusters from the tall palms. She pointed at the water-rushes along the edge of the pools. "We live like kings. When Pone well, we come back. Now what do you do, my man?"

Dondo spoke carelessly. "I go back to camp and help Buck McKee. I come back in three, four days."

"Let McKee and white man fight Frank LaWall, Dondo. The job is too big for one Ilak."

Dondo nodded seriously. "I do that, woman." He mounted Pone's horse and rode up the dim trail that led out of the pocket. But when he got out of sight, he did not ride toward the new dirt-camp—he swung to the east, going toward the N Bar S and Frank LaWall.

His eyes were shiny with hate. He rode fast then, pressing the jaded pony; the horse was tired, but game. The sun was lowering when he reached the rimrock east of the N Bar S ranch-house. He left his horse in some *chamiso* and went ahead on foot, carrying his rifle.

Lying on his belly, he watched the ranch below. Men were moving on the lower strata, going between buildings. He saw Frank LaWall three times, but the distance had been too far for rifle-work. Once he had raised his rifle and taken his sights, then he had lowered the piece unfired. With the great distance and the pitch and rise of the land he had little chance of sending a bullet through the red-headed man's huge body.

Darkness came, slowly.

Disgruntled, tired, he lay there, waiting for the N Bar S men to move out, to get on horses and head for Wildcat Dam. He had a touch of despair hit him. Pone lay back in the mountains, shot through the body—below him walked the man who had shot him. He saw Frank LaWall and Dusty Jacobson leave the bunk-house and go to the corral, where they stood on the far side, shielded from him by distance and the horses between them and the Ilak Apache, who lay there on the ridge with hatred in his heart.

Dondo gave his situation steady thought. With darkness here, he could not hope to shoot LaWall from a distance. There might be a chance to hide in the brush and drop the rancher as he rode past with his gunmen. But that would be plain suicide. The gunmen would run him down and murder him.

The two men—Jacobson and LaWall—could hardly be

seen now the night was gathering. While Dondo went for his horse, they stood there and talked. LaWall was in a bitter, sarcastic mood, and Jacobson did not like his tongue.

"Where in the hell is Jack Silsott, Dusty?"

"He's in the bunk-house. He'll be out, soon. He's oilin' his rifle."

LaWall studied the encroaching darkness. "We hit about midnight," he said. "Should be moonlight then. The powder is in a sack in the barn, tied to my saddle. Mink Black will fuse it when we get it set. He claims we just have to lay it on the upper part of the dam an' let it go."

"Mink should know. He was powder-monkey for the Southern Pacific when it built through the Wasatch mountains."

"He knows," said Frank LaWall.

The big red-headed man went to the bunk-house. Riders were dozing, old newspapers over their eyes to shut out the light from the kerosene lamps. They were ready for the trail. Jib Hobson lay on his side in his bunk, reading an old magazine. He looked up and Frank LaWall squatted beside him.

"All ready in here, Jib?"

Jib nodded.

LaWall got to his feet, running his glance around his men, mentally measuring them. Then he went to the house, thinking of the Apache he had shot the night before. Come morning, the Apaches would all be dead, he told himself. War Chief called from his bedroom as his father entered.

"Come on in, dad, and tell me a story."

"Not tonight, son."

"Why not?"

Frank LaWall looked in on the boy who lay under the hand-woven blanket, his black hair brushed back from his coppery half-breed face. "You be a good fellow, now, an' tomorrow night I'll tell you a long story."

War Chief considered that. "All right, I'll let you go at that, dad. Kiss me goodnight, huh?"

Frank LaWall kissed the boy and turned out the lamp. He stood there in the dark; his son slept. Feather Eagle was in her room, shuffling around, big and misshapen with her unborn child.

"Tomorrow I go to the mission, Frank."

"Tomorrow," he promised.

Now the moon was high enough. He heard the floor-clock inside strike ten. He went toward the bunk-house. Out of the shadows came Dusty Jacobson, spur rowels clattering.

"That time, boss?" asked Jacobson.

Frank LaWall said, "The hour is here, Dusty. You sound anxious."

Jacobson lit his cigarette. The flame of his stick showed his grooved, old-young face in relief. His eyes were almost closed against the brightness. He ran his thumb across the match and killed it; he broke it and tossed it aside. "Tomorrow, maybe, I won't see the moon, Frank."

"Hell, that dam will be unguarded."

Dusty Jacobson was silent. The night before, gunfire on the mountain had awakened him, pulled him out of his bunk. He had crouched, hidden, by the toolshed when Frank LaWall had ridden in. When Frank LaWall had been unsaddling, Dusty Jacobson had got to his feet and walked forward, spurs talking in the night. LaWall had turned, his gun out.

"Dusty comin', Frank."

"You're up late," growled LaWall.

"Shootin' on the mountain."

Frank LaWall had glared up at the peak. "Was up there in the rocks on guard. I shot an Apache. He was down here aroun' the buildings. One shot at me. I got the one I shot at."

"Kill 'em?"

"Wounded him. Think it was Pone. Dondo shot at me, I figure. I'll kill them two little hellions yet, Dusty. I got my horse an' rode back but I couldn't see nothin'."

"They left," said Dusty. "You're a damned fool, Frank. Ridin' back there! They could have holed up and knocked you from leather, you fool."

Dusty Jacobson took his thoughts from this. He went to the bunk-house and called in, "Rattle your hooks, cow-dogs. Tonight you earn your fightin' pay. Get your broncs and weapons an' we ride."

Jib Hobson grinned. "Plumb to hell, Dusty?"

"If the trail runs that way," murmured Dusty Jacobson.

Ten minutes later, mounted and armed, they left the

Basin, a string of horsemen riding into the foothills. Guards were out on either side. Dondo saw these take their positions, and he knew he could not kill Frank LaWall here. For if he did, his life would be worthless—they outnumbered him too greatly.

The Apache rode toward Wildcat Dam.

Now Wildcat Gulch lay below him. Moonlight shimmered and danced across the black, low wilderness. He settled down, patiently, and watched—he could not see the guards. He heard a man moving below him and he descended without sound, moving like a monkey downward, dropping from rock to rock.

He hid, looking at the man. Then said, "Buck," and went forward. Buck McKee had turned, hand on his holstered .45. He recognized the gnome and said, "Dondo, what is it?"

"LaWall, him come. Where guards? N Bar S guards?"

"We got them. One heard us and shot. We had to kill him. We moved in before the moon came up—went into position in the dark. I was up here scoutin' aroun'; thought maybe there might be another guard out, one we missed."

"There none." The leathery little face pinched in thought. "But what if no guard ride back—what if no guard meet Frank LaWall? Him suspicious then, huh?"

Buck considered that problem again. "Well, the guards were down low," he finally said. "He'd have ridden into our trap anyway, even if we hadn't got the guards—that is, if things had been normal, the guards had been stationed so close to the dam that LaWall would have ridden into our trap if he had got to where they were."

Dondo nodded, "I go back an' watch LaWall."

Buck looked over the moon-drenched pines and buckbrush. On the ridges and slopes were hidden his men with rifles. "I'll be down below by that big pine, there beside the rocks," he said.

"Me meet you there."

The little Apache was gone then, moving into the brush. Ten minutes later, high in the rocks, he watched LaWall and his N Bar S riders. Suddenly LaWall pulled in, his riders halting their mounts and ringing him in.

Dondo could hear what the big red-head said.

"Yonder, below us, is Mud Crick Dam. It ain't as big as Wildcat Dam, but we could blow it up, too. Or else, we could hit it alone, an' leave Wildcat for a later date, if needs be."

Dondo waited, heart pounding.

"We could do that," said Dusty Jacobson. "Save us some ridin', boss. Me, I don't cotton to this night work."

Jib Hobson spoke. "Dusty's lazy," he said. "Hell, that's only a pimple, compared with Wildcat. We got the cake in our hands an' we look at the bread."

"Jib's right," said LaWall.

And with Dondo drifting silently and unseen ahead of them, the N Bar S men rode toward Wildcat Dam.

CHAPTER 19

BUCK MCKEE did not look forward eagerly to the bitter task ahead. Nor, for that matter, did Tortilla Joe. After leaving Dondo, the tall cowpuncher went to the big pine tree, there to squat beside Tortilla Joe who sat stolidly on the ground, his back to the tree. The Latin's sloppy hat was low and he looked to be asleep.

"Wake up, damn you," growled Buck.

Tortilla Joe stirred. "Such language, Buck, to use to an ol' *amigo,* no? Me, I was not asleep—I was just storin' up my energies for the job ahead. How I wish I was ridin' across Mad Reever, headin' for ol' *Mejico* an' Santa Margarita by the desert."

"Humph...."

Buck squatted and chewed on a straw. He ran his eyes over the scene again, mentally marking the spots where his men were stationed. Janice had stayed in camp but Sin Braden was about fifty feet away, stationed with Colonel Henry S. Braden, who had promised to keep his mouth closed. The rest of the crew was placed in strategic positions behind rocks and *chamiso*.

"They ees come soon, Buck?"

Buck told him about meeting Dondo. Tortilla Joe dug into his pocket, came out with a *tortilla* wrapped in an old newspaper, peeled the paper back and bit into it. He ground the crust and beans between his molars. "Thees young fellow—thees Jeeb Hobson—I am afraid for heem."

Buck was serious. "Hope he gets out okay." He held his rifle on the small man who came through the brush, followed by a taller man. Then he lowered it when he recognized Dondo and Jib Hobson.

"They leave horses—they come on foot," said Dondo. "Me, I bring Jib."

Jib Hobson's face was pale under the bright moonlight. "I can't fire against them, Buck. They're dirty an' all that, but I rode with them—I can't lift a rifle against them."

"Go back to the new campin' grounds an' be with Janice," said Buck.

Jib Hobson turned and left. Dondo squatted and drew his knife. He whetted the long blade on his moccasin's sole. He ran his thumb along the edge gingerly. Then he took a straw, held it in one hand, hacked at it with the knife. The straw was cut instantly. He put the knife back in scabbard.

"Him sharp enough."

"Noise up yonder," murmured Tortilla Joe. Buck looked up against the far mountain. A man was moving down. Buck heard him call, "Carl, oh, Carl."

"Carl, him was guard," said Dondo.

Buck cupped his lips. "Here, you fool! Keep your mouth shut!"

"Everythin' clear?"

"All clear; keep quiet!"

They waited. Buck was tight inside. Tortilla Joe shifted, Dondo was silent. Now men were moving across the face of the dam. Buck said, "This is it," and got to his feet, walking toward the men who were on the earthen blockade. According to his orders, there was to be no shooting until he had called to the trapped N Bar S men, demanding they surrender.

But suddenly gunfire lashed out of the brush. A man screamed, went back, fell on the dam. Instantly all was commotion. Down there, N Bar S men were scattering, running, hollering. Buck cursed under his breath. The bullet had come from the place where Colonel Henry S. Braden had been stationed. He heard Sin Braden holler. "This damned ol' fool, Buck, he shot——"

Buck hollered, "Surrender, you men!"

His answer was a series of rifle bullets ploughing through the brush at him. He fell to a stoop, running ahead. Guns were talking against the mountains and the N Bar S men were retreating, firing as they ran for their horses. Cursing, the tall cowpuncher ran, heading them off.

The fight was short. Savage and ruthless, by its very nature it had deemed itself short-lived. Buck saw Frank LaWall running, triggered a shot, and missed. Then LaWall had run into the thick brush. Buck heard his boots pound up trail. Suddenly, a man crashed through the brush above him. He turned, his rifle up. But the man was Tortilla Joe.

"That loco colonel, he ees spoil all, no? But now eet ees too late—— I see Dusty Jacobson, heem run along down there!"

"Get to their horses," ordered Buck. "Keep them from gettin' to saddles!"

Lumbering, the Mexican broke the brush, heading for the higher rocks. Rifles and short-guns were spotting the night with scarlet flowers of flame. Buck hurried ahead, carrying his rifle. He wondered where Dondo was. His anger against the colonel had died.

Suddenly, he saw Dusty Jacobson. The man had just stepped into the trail, there about thirty feet away. He saw Buck and his Colt ran bright. Buck slid to a halt, mindful of Jacobson's bullet overhead, and he shot from that position, braced on one knee. His rifle bullets turned Jacobson's aim, knocking the man's bullets wide. Jacobson went to his knees, dropped his .45, and braced himself with his hands, standing on all four.

"Don't shoot, McKee," he said shakily.

Buck went to him. He kicked the man's .45 to one side. Jacobson fell down, and Buck knelt beside him. His bullets had hit the man high on the right ribs, and his shoulder sagged.

"Help me, McKee."

Buck knew he should have run ahead, going to the N Bar S saddle-horses. But he would be too late; already some of the N Bar S men were pulling out on horseback, whipping through the brush. He got his arm under Jacobson and moved him to a tree, putting his back against the rough bark.

Jacobson murmured, "Gracias, McKee," and his head

fell down on his chest. Buck got to his feet. He heard a man moving below him and he covered the brush with his rifle. Twenty feet away, Dondo came out into a clearing. The Apache knelt beside the grass and wiped his knife clean on its greenness, then he went on toward the dam.

The fight was over. Dim in the distance Buck could hear the beating hoofs of N Bar S men, retreating wildly. Dirt men and farmers were calling to each other and over it all was Colonel Henry S. Braden's bellow. Buck detected an edge of pain in the army officer's holler but disregarded it as he went down the slope.

There, in the brush, he found Frank LaWall.

LaWall lay on his back. Behind his left ear was a sharp, deep hole. Buck knelt beside him and saw that he was dead. The big red-head's grooved face had lost its hard lines, the simplicity of death had erased the marks of life. Buck had a feeling of loneliness, of deep reverence. He got to his feet and went to where Dondo had cleaned his knife.

Blood was on the grass.

Tortilla Joe came up and said, panting, "Buck, I theenk Frank LaWall got away! I theenk——"

Buck jerked a thumb back at LaWall's body. Tortilla Joe went to the man and looked down. He crossed himself and when he came back, his voice was husky. "A knife, she keel heem, no?"

"Dondo."

Tortilla Joe spoke slowly. "Death, she ees bad, Buck. But some mens you cannot do anythin' weeth, you has to keel them to make peace on the basin."

They went down to the dam. Two dirt-men came down, carrying Dusty Jacobson, who grinned weakly despite his pain. Another two came out of the brush toting Colonel Henry S. Braden, who grimaced terribly. Sin Braden was with them.

"What's wrong with that ol' fossil?" asked Buck.

"Shot in the leg."

Tortilla Joe asked, "His good leg or bad one?"

"His good one."

"Hate to be his nurse," said Buck. "Quite a chore, listenin' to that big mouth of his all the time."

A few of the dirt-men had been wounded, but none of them were killed. Two N Bar S men had been shot from leather, one killed. Buck stood on a high boulder. Below him, sleeping in pastorial simplicity, was Mad River Basin. And back at the N Bar S little War Chief lay in sleep, unmindful of the man who lay there on the mountain trail, his harsh face calm now in death.

The Mad River war was over.

The night-hawk rode ahead, getting Nappy Hale and the doctor, who met the cavalcade a few miles west of Oxbow. Old Nappy Hale issued orders, angry as a billy-goat stung by a hornet. He glared at Buck McKee.

"You in on this, McKee? Remember, you're on peace bond, fella!"

Buck smiled. "Me in on this ruckus! Nappy, how could you imagine such a thing! Ask Sin, she'll tell you!"

Sin smiled. "He was in bed, asleep, Nappy."

"Damned liars," growled the oldster. "Well, Sin, reckon you get your money back, then. Well, here we are at my office. Here comes Peta Gomez."

Peta did not see Tortilla Joe, who stood behind his horse. "My Tortilla," she said. "He ees not hurt, no?"

Tortilla nudged Buck. "Let's get out of here," he said. They led their horses into the alley. There Sin Braden followed them. Now that it was all settled, Buck said, they'd ride on.

Two months later, while drinking in a Santa Margarita *cantina,* a drifting cowpuncher told them about the final outcome of the Mad River war. Outside the warm Mexican sun washed over the sandy streets and caressed the rough 'dobe buildings.

"Nappy Hale had court the next day, I understand. He sentenced the N Bar S men to Yuma pen—that is, all they could find to capture."

"Some got away," murmured Buck.

"Yeah, an' if they got any sense, they'll never come back to Mad River, either. Them farmers are loaded for bear, Buck."

According to the puncher, Feather Eagle had taken the body of Frank LaWall over the *Sangre de Marias,* burying her white husband in the land of her people. She went back to the Indians, pushing aside her white conventions. War Chief, she said, would be an Indian.

Feather Eagle left the N Bar S with Nappy Hale for sale, and Nappy sold it to the farmers. They were cutting the range up. They were getting rid of the wild longhorn cattle and would raise white-faced Herefords on the graze. The last of the dams had been built and water now flowed in irrigation ditches.

"And Pone and Dondo?" asked Buck.

"Some claim that Dondo killed Frank LaWall, but nobody could prove it. Him an' Pone—he got well, you know—settled in their old village, there on the ridge over Mad River."

"An' Seen Braden?" asked Tortilla Joe.

Sin was boss of the Mad River irrigation project, with offices in Oxbow. Colonel Henry S. Braden was also in Oxbow. Loud as ever, he walked with a decided limp, a grim memento of his wound in the short and hectic Wildcat battle.

"Janice an' Jib Hobson got married. Right now, they're movin' into their new home a big log house built on the high back of Mad River. Dusty Jacobson went to the pen at Yuma. Well, reckon I gotta drift, Buck. Sin said that if'n I seen you boys, to tell you hello for her. That Peta woman, she bawled when she found out Tortilla here had left." The cowpuncher grinned.

"Let her howl," grunted Tortilla Joe.

The puncher left.

Tortilla Joe was studiously thoughtful. Finally he said quietly, "We dreenk to wild Mad Reever, Buck?"

There was a catch in Buck McKee's throat when he raised his whiskey glass. He was thinking of Mad River—of the surging, foam-tossed river that beat and fought against the rocks. He thought of the dead—and he thought of those who now lived in peace beside its roaring waters.

"To Mad River, *amigo mio*."

EXCITING WESTERNS FROM MACFADDEN-BARTELL

MONTANA MAN
by Paul Evan Lehman (50-256) ....50¢

NOTCHED GUNS
by William Hopson (50-252) ....50¢

SADDLE BOW SLIM
by Nelson C. Nye (50-247) ....50¢

THE MAN FROM THE BADLANDS
by Paul Evan Lehman (50-246) ....50¢

BOSS OF THE FAR WEST
by Burt Arthur (40-163)...........................40¢

BULLET-BRAND EMPIRE
by William Hopson (40-160) ....40¢

THE TOUGH TEXAN
by Paul Evan Lehman (40-159) ....40¢

HIGH POCKETS
by Burt Arthur (40-157) ....40¢

TROUBLE RIDES TALL
by William Hopson (40-154) ....40¢

BANDIT IN BLACK
by Paul Evan Lehman (40-152) ....40¢

SILVER CITY RANGERS
by Burt Arthur (40-151) ....40¢

GUN-WHIPPED
by Paul Evan Lehman (40-147) ....40¢

LONG RIDE TO ABILENE
by William Hopson (40-146) ....40¢

THEY RIDE WITH RIFLES
by Lee Floren (40-144) ....40¢

EMPTY SADDLES
by Burt Arthur (40-142) ....40¢

THREE GUNS NORTH
by Burt and Budd Arthur (40-140) ....40¢

SING A SONG OF SIX-GUNS
by Burt Arthur (40-138) ....40¢

FIGHTING RAMROD
by Lee Floren (40-136) ....40¢

THE DEPUTIES FROM HELL
by Chuck Martin (40-133) ....40¢

WOLF DOG RANGE
by Lee Floren (40-132) ....40¢

All books available at your local newsdealer. If he cannot supply you, order direct from Macfadden-Bartell Corporation, 205 East 42nd Street, New York, New York, 10017. Enclose price listed for each, plus 10¢ extra per book to cover cost of wrapping and mailing.